"Like I said, you... trouble. Maybe I can help."

The kid shuffles from foot to foot, shifty eyed. "Yeah?"

"Yeah. C'mon, kid—you act like you got a firecracker up your ass. I'm not a cop. Want a cigarette?"

The boy shrugs. "Sure."

Vince pulls a pack of Marlboros from his coat pocket and taps out a cigarette. The boy reaches for it. Vince brushes his hand aside and pulls out the butt himself. He reaches up and plugs it into the boy's mouth, holding it there an instant longer than he needs to, brushing his thumb against the boy's lower lip. The kid flinches, then stares up at the dark sunglasses as Vince pulls back to strike a match. He holds the flame six inches from the tip of the cigarette, making the kid reach for it.

"You look like you need a rest, kid. And a good meal. What's your name?"

"David."

"Yeah? Mine's Vince. Why don't you come to my place for a while? We'll catch a taxi...."

Also by
AARON TRAVIS
Slaves of the Empire
Beast of Burden

BIG SHOTS

AARON TRAVIS

BADBOY

Beirut was serialized originally in *Drummer* magazine, issues 121–124, September–December, 1988.

Portions of *Kip* ("The Hit" and "Vice") were serialized originally in *Stroke* magazine, issues 5/5 and 5/6 (1986) and issues 7/5 and 7/6 (1988).

Big Shots
Copyright © 1993 by Aaron Travis.
All Rights Reserved

No part of this book may be reproduced, stored in a retrieval system, or transmitted in any form, by any means, including mechanical, electronic, photocopying, recording or otherwise, without prior written permission of the publishers.

First BADBOY Edition 1993

First printing July 1993

ISBN 1-56333-112-8

Cover Photograph © 1993 Charles Hovland

Cover Design by Julie Miller

Manufactured in the United States of America
Published by Masquerade Books, Inc.
801 Second Avenue
New York, N.Y. 10017

BIG SHOTS

Preface 7

Beirut 11

Kip 73

PREFACE

Back in 1986, after doing a long, hard stint as fiction editor of *Drummer* magazine, I found myself unemployed. The bad news was that unemployment checks don't last very long, and starting up a freelance writing and editorial career is rocky business. The good news was that I had the free time and creative energy to get back to doing my own writing, something that being an editor seldom allows.

One of the first results was a story called "Getting Timchenko," which was as important a personal breakthrough for me as "Blue Light" had been when I was first starting out back in the late 1970s. (Both of those stories can be found in either of two anthologies, *The Flesh Fables: The Erotic Fiction of Aaron Travis*, published by Lavender Press, or *Flesh and the Word*, edited by John Preston, published by NAL/Dutton).

The other story that resulted from the release of my pent-up energies was quite the opposite of the sweet, tender "Timchenko": a nasty little item called "The Hit," which would be followed by a sequel, "Vice," both of which were serialized by *Stroke* magazine. A third installment, "The Big Shot," has never been published until now; even the anything-goes *Stroke* balked at publishing it. You'll find the whole story that began with "The Hit" at last collected here as a short novel under the title *Kip*.

"The Hit" was a breakthrough for several reasons. First, it marked the beginning of a period in which I would cut through many deeply internalized taboos about language and subject matter—and eventually come out on the other side. Which taboos? You'll see what I mean when you read these stories. Things can get pretty hairy when you let down all your psychological guards and confront your fantasies head-on, eyes open, fingers pressed to the keyboard.

"The Hit" also marked my first use of what I would come to call the "hyperthermal" mode: a way of writing as striking and powerful as I could manage. The hallmarks: third-person narrative plus present tense to give the action a cinematic immediacy; an utterly uncensored vocabulary; an obsessive sense of melodrama, guilt and retribution straight out of 1950s *film noir*. "The Hit" owes much to two specific films, *Carnival Story* (1954), with its unforgettable sexual dynamic between submissive, just-can't-help-it Anne Baxter and trashy Steve Cochran, and the more obscure *Murder by Contract* (1958), in which Vince Edwards, at the peak of his smoldering sexual allure, plays an amoral hit man. Indeed, there is a scene early on in *Murder by Contract,* in which Edwards humiliates an aging room-service waiter, which served as the germ of "The Hit"—except that the old waiter became beautiful young Kip.

Beirut was serialized originally in *Drummer* magazine. It continued the hyperthermal style in a modified vein. Like *Kip,* the idea behind it came from a late-show film—a nameless 1970s Z-movie about a

Preface

GI deserter on the lam in Vietnam who falls prey to a conniving black-market manipulator. Needless to say, the movie did not live up to its erotic potential, and so *Beirut* was born. Its theme is the young naïf who finds himself at the mercy of strangers in a foreign land, lost in the unexplored country of his own unthinkable appetites. In many ways, I have never been quite satisfied with this work. It goes perhaps too far; it reaches for forbidden fruit and falls from the precipice into darkness. Yet readers actually wrote to the editors at *Drummer* demanding a sequel!

Readers who remember my story "Crown of Thorns" may notice the guest appearance in *Beirut* of the Turks Rezi and Ahmed. They may also recall Sergeant Richter from a story called "Latrine Marine." Thus does the freedom of the hyperthermal mode allow all stories to melt into one.

And so *Kip* and *Beirut* share the pivotal character of Vince Zorio: hit man, black marketeer, big shot. While *Kip* might seem to take place in the 1950s, by necessity of the plot, it must occur after *Beirut*, which is set firmly in the early 1980s; the two stories are arranged here in that order. Yet, in truth, they take place in no time and at no place which ever existed, except in their author's unfettered imagination, and perhaps in your imagination as well, should you choose to read them. These tales take place in no particular order and with no strict logic between them, except for the unrestrained logic of the hyperthermal mode, in which all fantasies are allowed.

—Aaron Travis
Berkeley, 1992

BEIRUT

Beirut, Lebanon: 1983

I

The shop of Abdul the forger fronts one of the seamier bazaars of old Beirut. It has never been a pretty part of town; now the narrow streets are choked with high drifts of rubble and twisted steel. No sane man walks here at night; but during the day, a steady clientele files furtively up and down the dusty street: khaki-clad Arabs in burnooses with guns slung over their shoulders; Westerners wearing suits and ties, eyes shielded from the sun and hidden from sight behind black sunglasses. The street is the magnet of Beirut's underworld, a haven for black marketeers, gun runners, professional assassins, blackmailers, high-priced pimps and petty forgers. These are the only businessmen who still make a profit in a ruined city that once rivaled the cosmopolitan glamour of Monte Carlo or St. Tropez.

Vincent Zorio has been living in Beirut for almost

three months. He knows the street well. Having just finished a bit of import-export business in an office across the way, he pauses in front of Abdul's to light a cigarette.

Dust hangs heavy in the air, choking thick and hazy in the blinding sunlight. Suddenly the triple locks on the heavy wooden door to Abdul's begin to rattle. The door swings open. The first thing to emerge is the voice of Abdul's bodyguard, shouting in a staccato mix of Arab curses and broken English. Then a body shoots from the open doorway, like a stone catapulted from a slingshot. The heavy door slams shut.

The blond kid lands flat on his face. For a moment, he lies unmoving in the dust, then slowly picks himself up. Breathing hard. Shaking. Stooping to brush the dirt from his faded blue jeans and grungy T-shirt. At least he's alive, Vince thinks. Bodies don't always emerge from Abdul's in one piece.

Vince smokes his cigarette and watches, simply curious at first, but more and more interested the longer he stares. The kid looks to be in his early twenties. Very blond, his hair almost white in the bright sunlight—European, or more likely American, and probably a marine; his hair is a ragged, unkempt crew cut, like a grunt who's been letting his hair grow back. A marine's build, short but firmly packed with muscle. The kid fills out the T-shirt nicely. Very nicely. Vince feels a stirring at his crotch.

The kid looks up, suddenly realizing that he's being watched. Perhaps Vince misjudged his age at first glance. Sitting on top of the broad shoulders and muscular arms is a little-boy-lost face: soft coral lips, puzzled blue eyes. Blushing cheeks that have never seen a razor. Looking like an overgrown schoolboy who's just taken a tumble from the neighborhood bully.

Beirut

Vince leans against the wall and smiles. "Looks like Abdul doesn't want your business, kid."

The blond's eyes are wary. Taking in the shiny black shoes, the perfectly creased slacks, the broad, muscular mass of Vince's body inside the tapered coat. Finally looking up into the dark sunshades that give back his own dim reflection. He bites his lip, then turns and walks quickly up the street, threading his way through the crowd.

The boy is in a hurry, but Vince has a much longer stride. He follows at a medium clip, watching the boy's ass flex inside his tight jeans. At the corner of the street, he catches up with him, laying his hand on the kid's shoulder.

The boy swings around, backing into the wall. "What do you want?" His voice is a gasp, hoarse and high. Looking up at Vince with bright, scared eyes.

"Hey, kid, relax. I'm not gonna bite you."

The boy tenses. "You're American."

"Yeah. So are you." Vince looks down at the boy's chest, rising and falling in shallow breaths, noticing the way the loose T-shirt hugs his big pecs, the way his nipples push out against the thin cotton. "You must be in some sort of trouble, kid."

"Just leave me alone." The boy tries to bolt. Vince grabs his arm and jerks him back. Holds him steady, digging his fingers hard into the muscle, letting the boy feel his strength.

"I said relax. Catch your breath. Calm down." The kid stays tense for a moment, then slumps against the wall. Vince releases his arm, giving the plump, bruised biceps a friendly squeeze.

"Like I said, you look like you must be in a little trouble. Maybe I can help."

The kid shuffles from foot to foot, shifty eyed. "Yeah?"

"Yeah. C'mon, kid—you act like you got a firecracker up your ass. I'm not a cop. Want a cigarette?"

The boy shrugs. "Sure."

Vince pulls a pack of Marlboros from his coat pocket and taps out a cigarette. The boy reaches for it. Vince brushes his hand aside and pulls out the butt himself. He reaches up and plugs it into the boy's mouth, holding it there an instant longer than he needs to, brushing his thumb against the boy's lower lip. The kid flinches, then stares up at the dark sunglasses as Vince pulls back to strike a match. He holds the flame six inches from the tip of the cigarette, making the kid reach for it.

"You look like you need a rest, kid. And a good meal. What's your name?"

"David."

"Yeah? Mine's Vince. Why don't you come to my place for a while? We'll catch a taxi...."

Vince Zorio's apartment is located in the remains of a two-story stucco building in what was once a fashionable section of Beirut. Tall palms line the ruined boulevard. A latticework gate leads into a walled courtyard with a central fountain. The surrounding vines and shrubbery are long dead from neglect, the fountain dry and littered with scraps of debris. The structure once housed four apartments. Only two remain; the rest of the building was demolished by a stray grenade during a street battle a year ago. Vince is now the sole occupant. When he first moved in, a Christian doctor and his family lived in the rooms above; they packed for Paris more than a month ago.

As they step through the heavy door, Vince watches the boy's eyes widen in surprise. The interior is airy and modern: plush carpet, built-in appliances, air

Beirut

conditioning. The only sign of the explosion is a scorched circle on one wall where the fire almost broke through. Heavy drapes cover the windows, shutting out the bright sunlight, allowing no light to escape at night. The apartment has the cool detachment of a hidden sanctuary, cloistered and concealed from the broken world outside.

"When was the last time you took a shower, kid?"

David shrugs. "I don't know. A couple of days ago, maybe."

"Yeah, or maybe a week. You stink. The john's through there. Genuine German plumbing. Use all the hot water you want."

The boy glances over his shoulder, then disappears into the bathroom, closing the door behind him. Vince listens to the doorknob jiggle as the boy searches for a lock that isn't there. He makes himself a drink, then relaxes on the sofa. The pipes rumble beneath the floor; the shower comes on with a hiss. Vince reaches for the telephone.

For once the lines are working. It takes only a couple of calls to track the kid down. The grapevine confirms what he already suspected: the kid is hot. AWOL marine. Blond, 5'7', nineteen years old; PFC, full name David Jay Patowski.

Vince calls Abdul last. Abdul provides the twist. "He killed a man. Or at least he tried to. His own sergeant."

"Cold-blooded murder?" Vince glances at the door to the bathroom. "Maybe the marines trained him too well."

"Not murder. The sergeant lives. But I doubt the boy knows that. He leaves the man lying unconscious and bleeding from the head in a little bar called Cafe Fez near the American zone. It seems they fight over ... a personal matter. *Une querelle d'amour*. Though the attraction seems to have been one-sided. My informant sees them there before. Always out of uniform—Cafe Fez is off-limits to American personnel. All night the sergeant is touching the boy, cooing in his ear, forcing him to drink, handling him like a man handles a woman. Then the sergeant touches the boy in a certain private place. The boy swings around and strikes him with a bottle. Glass and blood everywhere. Then he runs from the bar. This is, oh, two weeks ago. My men see him everywhere since, but you know the Americans—they couldn't find the wart on their own ass."

"So the kid came to you looking for phony papers."

"Yes. Very nervous, very *amateur*."

"So why didn't you fix him up?"

"No money. I can't help every pauper and refugee in Beirut, Monsieur Zorio, even one as pretty as this. So I hint that I might take my payment in another way. Such a pretty ass, *n'est-ce pas*? Who could blame the sergeant who wants to touch it? The boy becomes most disagreeable. I would almost say hysterical. These American boys, such babies in matters of sex—not like you, of course, Monsieur Zorio."

"So you threw the kid out on his pretty ass."

"*Oui*. Rashid wants to take him into the back room and slit his throat, but I want no trouble with the Americans. And, if I may ask, what is your interest in this lonely young man, Monsieur Zorio?"

"That's my business."

"Of course. But I think he is not our type, eh? Allah alone knows how he survives for these two weeks, especially without selling himself. What does he eat? Where does he sleep? I would advise you, as one friend to another, to be careful."

Beirut

"Sure. I'm scared out of my pants." Vince smirks and hangs up.

The boy takes a long, hot shower. Long enough for Vince to silently enter the steam-clouded room and gather the rumpled jeans and T-shirt from the floor. In the bedroom he looks through the boy's pockets. A thin wallet, old and worn, molded to fit the curve of the boy's ass. Two twenty-dollar bills inside, a few Lebanese pounds, and some snapshots: Mom and Dad, a yearbook photo of a pretty brunette signed *All My Love, Diane*. David suited up for football practice, David in mortar board and robe at his high-school graduation, David posing with his rifle in dungarees, looking like a little boy playing soldier. A little boy with big muscles. The kid is damned good looking when he smiles.

Deep in the jangling front pocket of his jeans are a few Lebanese coins and some crumpled bills, petty cash. Reaching into the other pocket, Vince scoops out the boy's dog tag. The ball-link chain is tangled with another necklace, a little silver crucifix on a silver chain, engraved on the back: *David—Take Care. I'll Always Love You—Diane*.

The shower stops. Vince pockets the boy's belongings, then crumples the clothes into a ball and shoves them into a drawer. He sits in the chair beside the bed, kicks off his shoes and pulls out his pack of Marlboros.

He smokes two cigarettes before the boy finally musters the courage to step out of the bathroom. Vince listens to him shuffle around the living room. He takes a drag off the cigarette and smiles, feeling the anticipation. Feeling his cock thicken in his pants. The boy finally appears in the doorway.

His ragged blond hair is fuzzy and damp. The damp white towel around his waist is molded tight to his hips and thighs, showing the outline of his cock. His smooth, pale skin glows with a lustrous sheen after the hot shower, radiating heat, but he trembles as Vince looks him over.

There's a lot to see. The boy looks even better out of his clothes. He was a little chunky in the photos. Boot camp and two weeks on the lam in Beirut have burned off the last of his baby fat. Hunky is the word. Like a Polish plowboy. Broad, square shoulders. Muscular arms, perfectly smooth except for the vein that trails down each meaty bicep, and the mottled bruise left by Vince's grip. Strong, sturdy calves and thick forearms ending in wide, square hands and feet. Big, overhanging pecs that cast a shadow on his washboard stomach, capped by extra-large nipples, flat against the muscle and perfectly round. Vince watches them swell to the size of half-dollars as the boy's skin turns to gooseflesh in the cooler air.

"What did you do with my clothes?" The boy's voice is thin and small.

Vince takes a drag off his cigarette. He sits back in the chair, openly staring, feeling his cock stiffen and push down the the leg of his pants. He reaches down and gives it a squeeze.

"Where are my clothes?" The boy's voice became shrill.

Vince stands and walks across the room slowly. He raises the cigarette to his mouth. The boy flinches. Vince smiles. He isn't going to hit the kid. Not yet.

"I've been talking to some friends of mine on the phone. Word's out, kid. You're knee-deep in shit. Killed a man, didn't you?"

Vince smirks at the boy's reaction. Biting his lip, blushing like a girl. Shaking all over. Scared as hell. Two weeks in limbo have worn him to a frazzle.

"The marines want you back, Davy-boy. You

Beirut

know what they'll do when they find you? Lock you in a room and throw away the room. You'll be an old man before you see daylight again. And of course you know what happens to pretty young things like you in prison."

The boy sucks in a choking breath and begins to shake even harder.

"You're damned lucky they haven't caught you already. And even luckier you haven't been picked up by partisans. Those Arabs would love to get an American marine by the balls. Especially a pretty young blond piece with big blue eyes. And my guess is the State Department wouldn't exactly go out of its way to get you back, not after what you've done.

"You know what the locals do to war criminals? This ain't America, kid. Torture's an ugly business. They'll stretch it out for as long as you can last, then stretch it out a little longer. You're young. Strong. Just the kind they like. They can get a lot of mileage out of a kid like you. Take you apart piece by piece, starting with your eyeballs and ending with your asshole. Take pictures of what's left to send home to your girlfriend. Hell of a way to get on the cover of *Time* magazine."

The boy is chewing his lip, staring down at the floor, shoulders heaving on the verge of crying. Cracking even quicker than Vince expected. All marines are pussies at heart.

"You're five thousand miles from home, Davy-boy. Stranded in hell. Mommy and Daddy can't help you here. You haven't got a friend in the world—even old Abdul threw you out on your ass, and everybody knows Abdul's got a weakness for blonds. You should've pulled down your pants and bent that ass over his desk instead, like he wanted. You should've bent over for your sarge in the first place—saved yourself a lot of trouble—but it's too late for that. So instead you busted his head wide open in front of a dozen witnesses. Stupid cunt."

The boy is quaking now. At the the end of his rope. And why not—everything Vince says is true.

"What would you do with a phony passport, anyway? Any kid dumb enough to murder his own sergeant in the middle of a war zone can't have the brains to get out of the fix you're in. You're lost, kid. You blew it. Beirut is the end of the line. Your life is over before you've even had a chance to get started."

David looks up at him, eyes bright with tears. The kind of look that gives Vince Zorio a hard-on every time.

"But you said—you said maybe you could help me."

Vince nods. "Yeah. Maybe. But you haven't asked me yet."

The boy's eyes dart around the room, finally staring straight ahead at the knot in Vince's tie. "Please"—soft as a whisper—"please help me."

Vince flashes a crooked smile. "That's better. Of course, the kinda help you need costs a bundle. Phony papers, transport, safe housing for a known killer. That breaks about a dozen international laws to start with. Risky business."

"How much?" The kid looks up at him. Vince likes the expression—plaintive, helpless. He likes the way the boy's naked chest heaves up and down, showing off his big, glossy nipples. He feels his cock throb down his pants leg.

"Rough estimate—five grand."

David groans.

"Could be closer to ten." Vince shrugs. "How much have you got?"

The kid chews his lip. "A couple of hundred."

Beirut

Vince slaps him hard across the face. The boy looks up at him, dazed. Too rattled even to break and run.

Vince's voice is hard as steel. "I already looked through your wallet, kid. You got forty bucks and bus fare. Forty bucks'll buy you about five minutes of my time. You don't lie to me, kid. I'm the only friend you've got."

"But what am I gonna do?" The boy's voice cracks. The first tear breaks and slides down his cheek.

"You're gonna suck my cock."

The boy stares up at him. All the color drains from his face, leaving the smooth skin white as marble.

Vince smiles. "And a few other things. But you can start by wrapping those pretty lips of yours around my fat dick."

The boy steps back, shaking his head, staring down at the bulge in Vince's pants. "No, please, I can't …"

"A business arrangement, kid. You give me what I want, I get you out of this hellhole in one piece. It's your only chance, Davy-boy. That pretty mouth is about the only asset you've got. Probably not worth a damn, especially with a cock as big as mine, but I'll be the judge of that. I say we get started right now. Five thousand bucks adds up to a hell of a lot of blowjobs."

"But I can't—"

"Sure you can." Vince reaches for the towel and yanks it away. The moment is perfect, like a picture in a frame. The startled, frightened boy, cringing nude against the doorway, holding his hands in front of his crotch like a little girl. Mashing his big pecs together, deepening the cleavage, making the nipples stand out. David looks up at him, pleading with his eyes. Suddenly the pleading is gone, replaced by a desperate fury. The kid isn't broken yet after all.

"Give me my clothes!" Screaming and crying at the same time. "I'm not gonna suck your goddamned cock! I'm not a faggot! Give me my clothes!"

Vince resists the urge to slap him again. Instead he shrugs and walks to the dresser. He pulls out the crumpled T-shirt and jeans and tosses them at the boy's feet. "Get dressed. And get the hell out of here."

The boy fumbles with his clothes, bending over to pick them up, dropping them, picking them up again. Vince sits back in the chair and reaches for the bedside phone. The lines are still up and working. Allah be praised.

"Operator? Yeah, give me the American embassy ... Christ, when will these people to learn to speak English? American—embassy ... Yeah, *je comprends* to you too, sweetheart."

The boy freezes, bent forward in profile, one leg thrust into his jeans. The pose shows off the perfect curve of his ass and thigh. He stays that way, pretty as a picture, giving Vince something to look at while he waits for the call to go through.

"Yeah, who am I talking to? Well, Mr. MacIntosh, I believe I got a piece of vital intelligence for you. Never mind who this is. I understand you boys got an AWOL marine, PFC David J. Patowski." Vince pulls the dog tag from his coat pocket and reads the serial number out loud. "Yeah, that's the one. Blond kid, real pretty. Murdered his sergeant for trying to get into his pants. Damn right I know his whereabouts. I'm staring straight at him right now—standing in front of me naked, showing off his pretty ass.... Yeah, I'll hold." He covers the speaker with his hand. "Putting me through to some big shot. You're a hot potato, kid."

The boy knits his brow. Moves his lips.

"You say something, Davy-Boy?"

"Please—"

Vince cocks his head and squeezes the long thick ridge stretching toward his knee. "Yeah? Go on."

"Please don't. I—"

Vince holds the phone away from his ear. A tinny voice squawks from the speaker. "The man wants some answers, Davy-boy. So do I."

The blush is amazing to watch. It starts at opposite ends of the boy's body, coloring his forehead and feet, seeping inward to meet at his groin. He stares for an instant at Vince's crotch, biting his lip in dread. Shuts his eyes tight. Takes a deep breath that turns to a shudder. "I'll do it," he whispers.

"Do what? Speak up, kid."

"Suck your cock." His voice is thin and flat. Defeated. All resistance gone.

Vince smiles and nods. "I had a feeling you would. From the first minute I saw you." He lifts the phone to his ear. "Never mind, fartface. Private Patowski's about to give me a blowjob."

He hangs up and reaches for his zipper.

Vince sprawls in the chair, naked below the waist. His jacket and shirt lie strewn on the floor, along with his pants. The thin-ribbed T-shirt is rolled high above his navel, baring the hard, plated muscles of his belly, stretched taut across the broad, hairy expanse of his chest. He looks down between his legs, to the place where the boy's lips are mashed into his pubic hair, stretched thin around the base of his cock. Little Davy-boy is a quick learner.

He was pathetic at first. Shy of the big cock, having to be prodded every inch of the way. Vince found the right button to push almost by accident. He was getting the kid used to it, rubbing the big dick against his face, slapping him with it while he grilled him....

"You suck cock before?"

"No—"

"Don't bullshit me, Davy-boy. All marines suck cock."

"Never—"

"Not even your sergeant's cock?"

The boy's reaction was electric. Like a firecracker up his ass.

"Noooo!" A long, desperate whine.

"Yeah, but he wanted you to, didn't he? And instead you spilled his brains on the barroom floor. Stupid cunt. Here's your chance to make up for it. Just pretend that's the sarge's big dick. Go ahead, tell it you're sorry. Give it a kiss real sweet. Yeah, that's it. Now open your mouth and suck it inside. Make it feel good. That's what you're here for, cocksucker...."

The sarge was the ticket. Like a magic word—open sesame. Davy-boy swallowed him whole. Working hard for it. Impaling his face on the thick upstanding cock, forcing the broad head past the slick, tight ring of his throat, gagging himself on it and coming back for more. Punishing himself on Vince's big dick. Abasing himself on his hands and knees between the man's burly thighs. Vince looked down and saw that the kid's little weenie was standing straight up. An act of contrition ...

Vincent Zorio killed his first man at the age of twenty-two. Since then, he's killed a dozen more. Most of them for money. A couple for personal reasons. Nobody crosses Vince Zorio.

Vince has never felt the least twinge of remorse. A hit is a job; a job is what you do for a living. Vince is damned good at it—one of the best in the business—with a reputation that spreads from Beirut to San Francisco. Remorse is for the weak. Like Davy-boy. Vince has no sympathy at all with the kid's guilt, but Vince is willing and happy to exploit it. Guilt makes the boy weak and helpless. Guilt will keep him in his place. Like a handle for Vince to grab hold of and squeeze till he gets exactly what he wants.

He looks down at the tear-streaked face, plugged firmly to his groin by the thick core of meat speared down the boy's throat. He came in the kid's mouth minutes ago, but David still holds him tight. Eyes closed, trembling. Hands flat on the floor. His untouched little cock standing up hard as a bone.

Vince butts his palm against the boy's forehead and pushes him back, watching as inch after inch of glistening cock emerges from the clutching lips. The plump, meaty head pops free. The shaft bobs in the air, then rears upward, shiny and fat, as stiff as if he had never come. Vince is like that. It always takes more than one load to make his dick go down. The first round only takes off the edge; satisfying his cock a second time takes longer. He can go for hours before he shoots again, staying ramrod-stiff the whole time. That's why he saved the boy's ass for the second round.

David settles back on his haunches. Blushing all over, darting quick, disbelieving glances at the fat prong of meat that juts up from Vince's lap. Vince smirks at the way he holds his hands clumsily in front of his crotch, trying to hide his little hard-on. The only way to hide it would be to push it out of sight between the boy's legs. Not a bad idea …

Vince tilts his head. "You did that real good, Davy-boy. I'd say you're a natural-born cocksucker." He watches the boy hang his head and blush, then reaches over to pat the mattress. "Up, boy. On the bed."

David's face goes white. "Why?"

"Why do you think, cocksucker?" Vince grips his cock at the base, making it stand straight up. Waving it in the air. "I'm gonna screw your faggot ass."

"Please. No—" The boy cringes, staring at the cock, biting his lip in dread. "I'll suck it again—"

"You bet you will. After I've finished fucking you. Now up on the bed, belly down. I wanna find out if that ass if really worth dying for."

David groans, then crawls onto the mattress. Vince stands and pulls the undershirt over his shoulders. Walks to the dresser. Looks in the mirror to see the boy staring back at him over his shoulder, then burying his face in the pillows, embarrassed to be caught looking. Vince smirks and glances at his naked reflection. A big, broad-shouldered man, torso matted with dark, wiry hair. Cock jutting up from his muscular hips, hard as steel, shiny with spit, the slit still moist and leaking come. Big man with a big dick, about to fuck a naked blond marine. He reaches for the jar of Vaseline.

Vince struts around the room for a few minutes, lubing himself with a fistful of grease. Listening to the jelly crackle in the quiet stillness as he lathers it up and down his cock, making the thick, muscular shaft gleam in the dim light. Making the kid wait for it. He circles the bed, reaches for his pants and grabs the buckle end of his belt. The thin strip of leather slithers out of the loops.

The boy slowly lifts his head from the pillows. "What are you doing?"

"Just stay where you are, cocksucker. Grab the corners of the bed and hold on tight."

"But what are you gonna—"

"What does it look like I'm gonna do?" Vince stands beside the bed, coiling the belt around his fist.

Beirut

"You've been a bad kid, Davy-boy. What'd you do to get your old sarge so hot and bothered? Wiggle your ass at him inside those tight uniform pants? Shoot him shy little glances over your shoulder with those big blue eyes? Then bang him up the side of the head when he grabbed for it. And all the time you wanted it—bad. You're a born cocksucker from the word go, boy. The worst kind. Too bad for the sarge that you were too fucked up to figure it out on your own. Yeah, you've been a real bad boy. Bad boys need to be punished." He slaps the belt against the palm of his hand. "I'm just the man to do it."

The boy moans. Drawing his eyebrows together in a pained expression, staring upward. First at Vince's face, but only for an instant, unable to bear the hard glint in his eyes. Then at the belt, pulled taut between the man's meaty fists. Then at the big cock, jutting hard as steel from Vince's groin, greased and ready to fuck. He hides his face in the pillows and reaches for the corners of the bed, clutching the mattress in his fists.

Vince's lips curl into a thin smile. Just as he thought. He won't need ropes or handcuffs to give little Davy-boy the whipping he deserves.

"Hold on tight, cocksucker. Now spread your legs and pull your knees up. That's it, right alongside your chest. Belly down. Ass in the air. Give me a nice, wide-open target."

He stands beside the bed, staring down at the boy's body. Studying the curve of his upraised ass, watching the sweat break from his pores. Watching him flinch as he snaps the belt in the air, testing it. Vince raises his arm.

The blow lands with a sharp, meaty crack. The boy lurches forward with a yelp, clawing the mattress till his knuckles turn white, keeping his ass in the air.

Vince takes his time, making him wait for the second blow. Watching his body glaze with sweat. Listening to him moan.

The next blow is harder than the first. No holding back. The third is even harder. After the fourth, the begging begins. Just as Vince expected. The boy throws his head back, raises his ass high and starts to croak.

"Hurt me!" Clutching the mattress. Shivering in a cold sweat. Nude and glistening in the dim light, every muscle taut. *"Hurt me! Please!"* Thrusting his ass back, begging for the strap. Then shrieking as the belt strikes his flesh with a blistering crack.

The boy keeps asking for it. Vince keeps delivering. Fisting his cock with one hand, keeping it primed while he wields the belt with the other. Working the kid over until his ass glows cherry red, seething with heat. Putting the full strength of his arm into every blow. Working up a sweat. Getting drunk on the rhythm of leather striking naked flesh. Hardly noticing as night falls and the room grows dark.

He walks to the dresser. Lights a candle. Looks at the boy's reflection in the mirror—trembling with exhaustion, still holding the pose. Face pressed against the headboard, ass raised high. The bedsheets wildly rumpled and damp with sweat. Vince moves to the foot of the bed. Listens to the boy beg. Draws back his arm. Aims for the boy's hole.

The tip of the belt strikes the pouting lips dead center.

A crack like pistol fire, followed by a keening howl. For a strange, unreal instant, the boy levitates clear off the bed, then crashes back to the mattress, jerking in a violent convulsion that sends shock waves through the floor. Vince sucks in his breath. The boy is coming.

Beirut

He throws the belt aside and mounts the bed. Positions his greasy cock at the mouth of the boy's virgin hole. Drives the shaft all the way home with a single gut-wrenching thrust.

The boy goes rigid, but his hole is alive, contracting in time with his spurting cock—squirming, squeezing, swallowing the huge dick in a series of spastic convulsions. Vince pulls his cock all the way out, then spears the boy to the hilt, matching his high squeal with a grunt.

Vince grabs the boy's hips and begins to pump, settling in for a long, hard screw. The shrieking subsides to a breathless whimper through gritted teeth. "Yes—hurt me—please. Punish me—fuck me, sarge...."

▌▌

"No—Please—"

David's voice is small and hoarse, hardly more than a whisper. He stands in the center of the dingy little office. Head lowered, hands tied behind his back, shivering. Nude, except for the tiny pouch that holds his genitals. His body glistens with a thin sheen of nervous sweat. He stares down through half-shut eyes at the shiny black shoes of the stranger who stands before him.

Vince stands behind him, one hand on David's shoulder, the other holding the chain attached to the collar around David's throat. "Go ahead, Davy-boy." Vince's breath is warm in his ear. "Show the man what you're good for."

He squeezes David's shoulder hard, then brushes

his fingers down the boy's back, tracing the silky cleavage of his spine. Skin like pale satin, slick and shiny with sweat. He opens his big, meaty hand and cups it around one of David's naked buns. The taut, smooth skin turns to gooseflesh as he fondles it. Vince spreads his fingers and grabs a fistful of ass. Squeezes hard. The soft white flesh plumps up red in the gaps between his fingers. David responds with a whimper.

The squeeze relaxes. The fingertips brush delicately over the mottled skin, then tighten into a sharp, sudden pinch that makes the boy jiggle. Vince smiles. He weighs the taut, springy flesh in his palm again, gives it a hard slap, then slides the edge of his hand into the slick, sweaty cleavage and strokes the hole with his middle finger.

David's mouth opens in a ragged gasp. His face and chest and the milky flesh between his thighs blush bright red as he breaks out in a fresh sweat. Vince has never used him in front of another man.

David shuts his eyes tight. *"Please—no—not here—not like this ..."* His hole begins to quiver. He tries to will it shut, but the conditioning runs too deep. The tender, moist ring of flesh oozes open, pushing inside out, grasping like a sucking mouth until it swallows Vince's finger to the second knuckle.

Vince twists the boy's hair into a knot, forcing him to lift his face. For an instant, David glimpses the stranger. Not an Arab, as he had expected. Dark, Italian, middle-aged. Broad shouldered and soft around the middle, like an older, heavier version of Vince. Tall and burly, dressed like Vince in a black suit and tie. The man's features are large and blunt, brutally handsome. A neatly trimmed mustache bristles above his broad upper lip. He leans against a desk cluttered with photographs. One hand holds a cigarette. The other hovers near his crotch. The big man leers at him, curling his upper lip in a thin, crooked smile.

Vince yanks hard at the fistful of hair, pulling back until the boy's chin juts toward the ceiling. The stranger drops from view. David stares upward at the network of grimy black pipes that crisscross the ceiling above. Suddenly Vince slides his middle finger all the way home, screwing and jabbing until the boy is forced squealing to his toes. The ceiling goes blurry. Tears run down the sides of his face, gathering at his earlobes. They fall in a straight line onto the dimples above his ass. His hips break into an automatic grind, riding the finger thrust up his hole.

Vince croons in his ear. "Yeah, that's more like it. Do your dance for the man, cuntboy. That's what we wanna see.... Come on, throw your chest out. Show the man your titties."

David squares his chest, clasping his bound hands together, knotting his shoulders, ramming his fists into the small of his back. Vince slips his finger from the hole with a liquid pop, then teases it, pinching and pulling and scraping his fingernail against the tender lining.

David strains backward with his hips, craving the finger. Chin up, shoulders back, torso stretched like a bow. The finger pokes playfully at his hole, then pulls out of reach. Vince chuckles in his ear. "Yeah. Pussyboy needs a finger up his hole, huh?" Vince jerks hard at the fistful of hair.

"Yes!" David blushes pink from head to toe.

"Then reach for it. Give it a kiss."

David whines and spreads his legs, still on tiptoe, twisting his heels and thighs outward until his ass is wide open, his muscular buttocks flattened, his hole completely exposed. He strains, and the moist inner lining of his tube distends, pushing outward like a blossom, pink and slick like the inside of a mouth.

Vince gives the puckered lips a playful swat, hard and stinging. The hole contracts for an instant, then pushes out again. Vince gives the hole another hard slap, then slides four fingers inside. David goes rigid, snorting like a horse.

"Well, Benny?" Vince cocks an eyebrow. "What do you think?"

The man takes a long drag on his cigarette. He wears a poker face, pretending to be unimpressed. The hard ridge down his pants leg tells another story. His hand inches a little closer to the bulge, fingers twitching.

He finishes his cigarette and flicks it to the floor. Grinds the butt into the concrete, then lights another. Taking his time, still wearing the poker face. He pushes himself off the desk and steps forward.

David jerks as he feels the man's touch on his face. The big, calloused hand caresses his smooth, beardless cheek. David tries to pull away, but the fingers up his ass hold him in place. The man cups his jaw, pushes his head even farther back, squeezes his mouth open. He runs his thumb over the moist pink lips, then slips his thick middle finger inside. David shuts his eyes tight and clamps his lips around the man's finger, sucking at it like a cock. The finger tastes of tobacco and sweat. Fingers up his ass. A finger in his mouth. Plugged at both ends, like a chicken on a spit.

The man finger-fucks his mouth casually, sliding his fingertip over the gums and tongue, probing David's throat until he gags. Saliva bubbles around his lips, running over his cheeks and down his neck.

The man pops his finger free. He slides it over the boy's chin, probing the soft tissue beneath his jaw.

Beirut

David's throat bulges from his neck, a wide tube clearly defined beneath the taut flesh. The man squeezes it gently between his forefinger and thumb, prompting an involuntary swallow. The soft tube spasms, rippling like a caterpillar beneath his fingers.

The man takes a quick deep breath. "Good-looking throat. Bet you can pack a big one down that hole." Vince smiles and starts to fuck his fingers in and out of the asshole, keeping the boy primed. He glances down at the bulge in the man's crotch and smiles. Benny is hooked.

And why not? Even though he stands behind the boy, Vince knows exactly what the man is seeing. He's seen it himself, plenty of times before. David is locked in Vince's favorite pose. Straining on tiptoe, his trembling thighs splayed wide open. Ass impaled, head thrown desperately back, hands tied, thrusting his chest forward and stretching his belly taut.

The boy has a spectacular physique—a hard, square frame covered with a thick padding of smooth muscle in all the right places. Broad shoulders, narrow hips. Short, muscular limbs, big pecs, an ass like a split melon. Skin pale and flawless as a baby's. The pose shows him off at his finest, the very picture of submission and craving: a blond muscleboy in bondage, flaunting his big tits, putting his fuckholes on display.

This is the way Vince likes to make him stand before he gives the boy a long hard screw—except that instead of his fingers it would be a buttplug up David's hole while Vince circled him slowly, making him wait for it, letting the craving build until he crashes, letting it build again. Whipping his ass with a belt, pinching his big nipples. Punching his belly, slapping his cock. Twisting the buttplug up his hole. The boy hates to beg for it. He always does, by the time Vince is through with him.

Benny's poker face begins to crack. He licks his lips, takes a quick drag off the cigarette. He runs his finger down the hard cleavage of the boy's chest, to the shallow navel surrounded by plates of scalloped muscle. "Naturally hairless?"

"He is now. Permanently."

David didn't have much hair on his body to start with. Electrolysis took care of the rest. Vince chuckles, remembering the way the boy wriggled under the needle. Five sessions spread over five days, three hours a session. The specialist charged an arm and a leg, but it was worth it to watch the boy strapped down on the leather cot, writhing as the needle denuded him completely below the neck. First the stocky, muscular legs, with their fleecy dusting of fine blond hair. Then the soft wisps around the boy's nipples and under his arms. Then the sleek, glossy pubic patch that ran from belly button to crotch and on between his legs to swirl softly around his hole.

All hairless now, forever. The specialist wouldn't do the kid's balls. Vince took care of that himself, plucking out the silky blond strands one by one.

"Smooth as silk all over, just the way you like 'em." Vince saws his fingers in and out of the boy's hole, pumping air into the pocket, listening to it fart around his fingers. "No more shaving. Nothing left to shave. Just wait till you feel your dick up his smooth hairless hole."

The man licks his lips, openly squeezing the bulge in his pants, staring at the boy like a hungry wolf. His voice is dry and tight. "Yeah ... I can see. You've done quite a job on his nipples, too."

David's nipples are Vince's special creation. The same specialist who denuded the boy's body adminis-

Beirut

tered the silicone. A single injection of viscous jelly into the tiny cavity beneath each nipple, pumping them up like tiny balloons. David had extra-large nipples to begin with, perfectly round, like copper medallions pressed flat against the boldly curving contours of his pecs. Now they stand out almost an inch from his chest, obscenely bloated cones of flesh perched at the tip of each pectoral, tender and glossy, amazingly resilient to the touch. Nipples as shiny smooth and sensitive as the tip of a swollen penis, perpetually erect.

The nipples have a freshly molested appearance, puffy and pink, shiny with saliva. Vince likes to suck on them for hours at a time while his dick is planted up the boy's fuckhole, clamping his lips around the base and sucking each bud into his mouth, feeling them swell up to ten times their original size. Sucking until they ache, nibbling and teasing his tongue against the tender tips, reducing the boy to his most shameless state of craving. Sucking the boy's oversized nipples while the boy's hole sucks his oversized cock.

Benny licks his lips and raises the cigarette to David's chest, bringing the glowing tip within a hair's breadth of each plump, protruding nipple, watching the boy's pectorals contract, listening to his breath grow ragged.

"Easy," Vince says. "Careful with his titties. He's not yours yet."

The man steps back. The poker face is gone. In its place is a mask of raw lust. He stares at the boy's crotch. "So where's his dick?"

"Why, you think he needs one? The kid's already got a pussy between his legs."

"C'mon Vince. I wanna see the whole package."

Vince chuckles. "Sure. Just pull the string. But there's not much to look at."

David's cock and balls are hidden from sight, packed tightly together inside a soft suede drawstring pouch. The mouth of the pouch is tied so tight around the base of his genitals that it hardly seems attached. It bobs ludicrously between his legs, a small leather ball stuck to the nude delta of flesh where his thighs and belly converge. With his penis and testicles compacted so tightly, concealed and camouflaged in the pouch, it's easy to imagine nothing at all between his legs except a smooth, sleek depression leading back to the fuckhole between his cheeks.

The man finds the string and tugs at it, then pulls the pouch away. David shudders and gasps as his cock unbends and straightens fully erect for the first time in days. It snaps up against his belly, rigid and quivering, pointing toward his navel but reaching only halfway. Short and stubby, bone-hard. Slender whip marks show on the taut, translucent flesh, more whip marks at the blunt, moist tip. A toy cock, the most sensitive kind, all the nerve endings packed close together. Stripped of the surrounding pubis, it juts up nude and vulnerable from the boy's groin, like a squat little whipping post. Useless for fucking. Perfect for punishment.

"Yeah." The man snaps his finger against David's cock and sniggers. "Not much in the weenie department. But his eggs look like they might be fun to crack." He narrows his eyes and reaches down to cup the hairless testicles in the palm of his hand. Fat, heavy balls, plump with unspent semen. The most sensitive kind, painfully full of come with no place to unload. The man squeezes. The balls vibrate in his hand like gelatin.

Benny steps back and leans against the desk, almost tripping, unaware of his clumsiness. All his attention is channeled forward in an unblinking, smoldering stare. Vince nods. The corner of his mouth twists into a smirk. He pulls his fingers from the boy's hole with a loud, smacking *pop*. David bleats, whines. A fresh sheet of sweat pours down his chest.

"Jesus, Vince. How do you do it? Don't tell me the kid came to you this way."

"The kid came to me a virgin. Never been porked. I just gave him a taste of my kind of loving. Soon as he found out what a real dick could do to that pussy-pot between his legs, he forgot all about that little nub in front. You could say we came to a quick and mutually satisfying understanding." Vince laughs—not at his own words, but at the twitch that flutters at the edge of Benny's mouth and the beads of sweat popping out across his forehead.

Vince takes a quick look at the nude and straining body beside him. David senses the glance. The veins bulge from his neck; his hips sway back, fucking the air.

Vince delivers a stinging downward slap to the boy's dick. "Put your little toy away."

David hunches forward, opening and closing his thighs. It's a move he's obviously performed many times before. Without using his hands, he manages to tuck his hard cock between his legs, then squeezes his thighs together and stands upright. Nude. Sexless. Nothing showing between his legs but his smooth, bald crotch. He draws his eyebrows together and shuts his eyes in shame.

Benny stares. His mouth hangs open. The breath rattles in his throat. "I gotta fuck him. Now."

"Sure. We can talk business after. Right here?"

"Over the desk."

The man steps out of the way, unbuckling his pants hurriedly as Vince pushes the dickless boy forward, bending him over the desk, smirking with approval at the way the moist, slick hole automatically opens in a kiss.

David's face is pressed into the clutter on the desk. An inch from his nose, grotesque at such close range, is a glossy photo of a pretty redhead, his mouth impaled on a huge cock, his bright blue eyes gazing up at the camera in astonishment. David stares at the picture for an instant, then jerks as something thick and blunt begins to slide between his cheeks. He feels his hole yawn open with a will of its own, welcoming the intruder, reaching for it. He can't seem to squeeze it shut, no matter how hard he tries. He shuts his eyes tight and begins to cry again....

Fifteen minutes later, Benny is seated in the swivel chair behind his desk, smoking a fat cigar. Pants around his ankles. Shirt open, chest hairs glistening with sweat. His big chest pumps up and down slowly, as he catches his breath. A quick, hard fuck. Next time he slams the kid, he'll take his time, draw it out, really put the boy through his paces. This time he was just too hot. Vince's fault—Vince really knows how to show off the goods. And the way the boy squealed, even while his asshole was gobbling dick like a hungry mouth—nobody knows how to train a piece of boycunt like Vince Zorio.

David is on his knees between the man's burly thighs. Face buried in his crotch, lips stretched thin and mashed flat against the wiry patch of hair that sprouts at the base of Benny's dick. The thick, greasy tube of flesh is buried down his throat, pulsing and warm. After the fuck, Benny said he wanted to soak his dick for a while before getting down to brass tacks. Vince was happy to oblige.

David's hole is burning and raw at the mouth, pummeled and bruised inside. Benny has a big one.

Beirut

His ass is red and welted, marked with handprints. Benny is a hitter. His hole, gaping and loose after the hard fuck, suddenly lets out a long, rasping fart. The big load Benny pumped up his ass begins to backflush, dribbling down the inside of his thighs. Above him, the men laugh. David's ears blush dark red as he cuts another fart, helpless to stop it.

His hands are still tied behind his back, his cock still tucked out of sight between his legs, hard as a pipe, riding the ridge that leads back to his hole. Benny reaches down with one hand, cupping his smooth, meaty breasts, plucking at the pumped-up nipples. David groans around the dick in his mouth and squeezes his stubby cock between his thighs, rubbing the denuded, sweaty planes of flesh together, rolling his hips. He could come that way. It's the only way Vince lets him come. The fuck has left him hot and aching for it. But David knows better. He stops at the first twinge of pleasure between his legs, then concentrates on the fat, satisfied dick in his mouth, stroking it with his tongue, squeezing it with his throat, trying hard to make Benny feel good.

The man rewards him with a sharp slap across the face. "Not so hard, cocksucker. I told you, nice and slow. Nice and easy. You suck the way I tell you to suck.... Yeah, just let it slide down your throat. That's the ticket, kiddo." The man takes a long drag on the cigar, then blows a cloud of smoke into David's face. David chokes and coughs around his dick. Benny clenches his teeth at the unexpected pleasure.

Vince sits with one knee propped over the corner of the desk, casually leafing through a stack of photos. Most of the models are Arabs. Smooth, slim-hipped bedouin boys with long lashes and tender nipples. Big, hairy-chested Arabs with dark mustaches and thick circumcised cocks. He pauses when he comes to a batch he hasn't seen before. Two musclemen, Turks by the look of them, working over a nude and obviously reluctant redhead. A new boy; Vince has never seen him before. New to Benny's establishment, new to the game; the look of astonishment on his freckled face is too genuine to be phony. Fresh meat. A meeting can be arranged, as always. Vince will make it part of the deal. He'll be needing a fresh hole to unload in while David is in hock.

"So, Vince." The man's voice is cloudy with smoke. "Where'd you find the kid? A fucking blond, no less. Must be a long way from home."

"American," Vince says. "Small-town boy. Ohio born and bred."

"So what the fuck's he doing in this hellhole?"

"What do you think?"

"Looks like a marine."

"Yep."

"So how the hell did you get your hooks into him?"

"Ran into him outside Abdul's."

"AWOL, huh? Kid trying to score a phony passport? What's the story?"

"What's to tell? The kid wants to go home. I offered to help. Of course, these things cost money ..."

"And you don't take charity cases."

"He's been earning his keep. But he'll have to earn a hell of a lot more if he's ever gonna pay his way home. Transit, safe housing, new identity. The works. I figure the best way for him to bring in some big bucks fast is doing a few months at your place."

Benny makes a face. "Business, with the war, it ain't what it used to be."

"Come on, Benny. A blond American, in this place? With his kind of body? You know your regulars will pay big bucks for a crack at his ass. He's prime stuff."

"Well ..."

Vince takes a final look at the cute redhead, then tosses the photos on the desk. He reaches into his coat pocket for a cigarette, looking down at the boy's upthrust ass. He swings his foot forward and pokes the tip of his shoe into the sweaty crack. David hunches back, groaning around the cock in his mouth. His asshole yawns open and swallows Vince's foot to the instep, drooling a mass of slick semen onto the shiny leather. Shoeshine boy, giving him a hot-wax job with his ass. Vince will have him buff the tops with his tongue before he leaves.

Vince lights the cigarette, whips the match through the air, and tosses it onto David's ass. The hole snaps tight around his foot. Benny sighs at the squeal that vibrates through his cock.

Vince takes a quick drag off his cigarette and exhales. "We'll work something out ..."

III

"I told you already—I had a blond in mind." The customer's voice is stern and deep, his patience wearing thin.

"Blond," Benny mutters, squinting as if he's never heard the word before. "Blond, huh? You sure? Redheads can be a lot of fun." He flashes his best used-car-dealer smile. "And this number's got a beautiful hole. A real honeypot. I guarantee from personal experience." He gropes himself and sniggers.

Benny and the customer stand in a darkened hallway in front of a long one-way mirror, peering into the dimly lit cubicle beyond. Benny has already shown him the Arab boys. The man threw a boner in his pants you could spot across a football field, but claimed he wasn't interested. Kept talking about a blond. Benny saved the redhead for last. After the Arab boys got the big guy frustrated and hot, maybe the redhead would do.

The redhead's name is Duncan. Belfast boy, barely eighteen. Like all Benny's boys, Duncan has a story. Got tired of being spanked by the nuns at Catholic school, skipped town, and made his way to Liverpool; stowed away on a German freighter because he wanted to see the world—but ended up seeing not much more than the four walls of the captain's cabin, and a lot of the captain's dick. Four months at sea chained nude to a bare metal cot made him long for the milder touch of Sister Agnes's leather strap. One night three of the swabbies broke in and raped him; the captain called it "cheating" and kicked him off the ship in Beirut without a penny. That was when Benny got his hooks into him.

Duncan is slender but sturdy, with a lean, coltish body—long arms and legs, a tightly muscled chest. Skin like peaches and cream. Cute face with freckles and an upturned nose. He lies naked on the bed, exhausted and dozing, curled into a ball with his backside toward the mirror—just back from an overnight loan-out to Benny's friend Vince Zorio. Naked, that is, except for the dog collar around his throat and the leather cuffs with D-rings around each ankle and wrist; Vince didn't even bother to take them off. Broad red stripes across the boy's ass show where Vince has been using his belt.

Benny raps on the glass, then growls into the

speaker. "Rise and shine, cocksucker. You got another customer."

The boy jerks on the bed, then lets out a low whimper. He unfolds his long limbs, groaning as if he's too weak or too stiff to move. He slumps onto the floor and crawls toward the mirror on his hand and knees. All Benny's boys are trained to obey without question. All Benny's boys know how to crawl.

Duncan reaches the mirror. Benny looks down through the one-way glass and sniggers. "Stand up, kid. Give the man a look."

The boy rises awkwardly to his feet. Wobbly as a newborn colt, trembling at the knees. Eyes dull and glazed. He looks into the mirror, flinching at his own reflection.

The corner of his mouth is swollen and bruised, his cheek welted with the outline of a handprint. His nipples are distended and puffy, standing out from his hard, lean chest like ripe strawberries—a night with Vince Zorio. His cock, surprisingly big on such a slender frame, curves up stiff and rubbery, as red and swollen as his nipples, laced with slender whipmarks. As usual, Vince didn't let him shoot.

The customer frowns. "Doesn't look too fresh."

"Don't worry," Benny says. "You know these young fags. Lots of pep. Just look at his dick—hard as a rock."

"I'm not interested in his dick."

Benny leans toward the speaker. "Turn around, kid. The man wants to see what you're good for."

The redhead looks unhappy. He bites his lip, lowers his eyes. He begins to shake, and his hard, lean chest breaks out in a sweat.

"Turn around, kid." Benny's voice is low and menacing. "Show the man your pussy."

The boy takes a shuddering breath, then slowly

turns and bends forward at the waist. He grabs his ankles and rises on tiptoe, spreading his cheeks wide open.

Red stripes show where Vince's belt licked all the way into the boy's crack, nipping at the hole. The little bud shows all the signs of having been freshly fucked by a very large cock—the pink lips are raw and chafed, swollen like a bee sting, shiny with oil and semen. As they watch, the hole yawns open, pooching outward like a mouth puckering for a kiss, oozing inside out to expose a half-inch of the slick lining within. The hole begins to flutter and fart, dribbling a stream of gooey semen, smacking its lips with a soft, popping noise if it were trying to speak. The unmistakable mark of the master—*Vince Zorio was here*. An educated fuckhole, trained to beg out loud for cock, custom fitted to give maximum pleasure to an oversized dick.

"What'd I tell you? Quite a hole, huh?" Benny gives the upthrust ass a dreamy look. "Kinda makes you wanna stick your finger in it." He glances down at the customer's crotch. The bulge is still there. So is the stony expression on the man's face.

"Too skinny. I told you I wanted a blond. A blond kid with some meat on him."

Benny wrinkles his nose. One-time clients are a pain in the ass. Always showing up with something particular in mind, waving a fistful of cash, wanting it right away. Of course he can't blame the guy for being picky—not at the rates Benny charges. The cost of a good time has gone up since things starting falling apart in Beirut.

The good old days. Only a few years ago, Beirut was the center of the world. Like Havana in the fifties, until Castro and the revolution came along to spoil the fun. Beirut has the war with no winners; no perfect setup can last forever. Benny will have to move his operations soon, but not until the regulars have coughed up their last dime and even the rats start evacuating the rubble.

Benny sighs. "Okay. Tell you what, I still got one possibility. But he won't be fresh. He's busy taking care of a couple of clients right now."

"So what are you waiting for?"

Benny shrugs. The customer is always right.

They turn and walk down the hallway, leaving Duncan bent over with his ass in the air, confused but afraid to move, his legs trembling from the strain, his cock-hungry hole smacking its lips.

Benny leads the man to the end of the corridor, then down a flight of booming metal steps. The basement is warm and humid, like a steambath. The hallway is so narrow that the two men walk single file. Naked light bulbs hang from the ceiling; patches of darkness alternate with cones of harsh white light. The walls and floor are painted black. Metal pipes crisscross overhead, covered with a crust of fuzzy grime.

As they round a corner, Benny gives the customer a sidelong glance. Despite his blond features and a faint southern accent, the man reminds him somehow of Vince Zorio. The same hard set of the jaw. The same surly curl on his upper lip and the smarmy, condescending look in his pale gray eyes. The same hard bulge at the man's crotch, extending halfway to his knee. Handsome as the devil and hung like a horse, and well aware of it. A big guy, big all over, filling out his casual linen suit like a football player turned fashion model.

At least Vince Zorio has a sense of humor. Vince can roll with the punches; of course Vince is the one who does the punching. But the blond southerner is no good ole boy. His bearing is ramrod stiff, aristocratic and aloof. No nonsense. Strictly business. Military, maybe, West Point, or some big-shot young executive, the kind of go-getter who makes it hard for the older exec.s to sleep at night. The kind of man who doesn't take no for an answer.

They round another corner and stop in a patch of darkness, facing a wall covered by heavy drapes. From beyond the drapes come muffled sounds of grunting and the heavy, sweaty crack of flesh against flesh. Benny draws back the curtains to reveal another one-way mirror.

"The only blond I got in stock right now." Benny lights a cigarette. "The clients are a couple of Turks from Istanbul. Rezi, the big one, and his buddy Ahmed. Get down to Beirut three or four times a year. Always know they'll have a good time at Benny's. I give 'em a discount. They help keep the boys in line."

The little cubicle is furnished sparsely. A small bed, a night stand, an easy chair, a seedy carpet with an arabesque pattern, its colors dim and faded. A shaded lamp with tassels gives off a lurid amber glow.

Ahmed is seated in the chair, stripped down to a grungy white T-shirt. Slumped low in the seat, knees hooked over the padded arms, exposing his genitals and the hairy crack of his ass. Every inch of flesh between his thighs is covered with a thick, glossy coating of spit. The moist bud of his asshole glistens with saliva in the amber light.

His big cock is slung forward, drooping down, the head nestled between big low-hanging balls. Thick and bloated, with the swollen, rubbery look of a big cock that's been sucked on for hours. A cock that's already come more than once, resting before it comes

Beirut

again. A thread of leftover semen dangles from the tip.

Ahmed's eyes are half-shut and dreamy. Beneath his perfectly trimmed mustache, his lips are curled in a faint smile of amusement as he watches the show....

In the center of the room, in profile to both the sleepy Turk and the unseen watchers beyond the glass, a hunky young blond is naked on his hands and knees. The other Turk—the giant, Rezi—is seated on the boy's lower back, riding him like a pony across the room.

Rezi is a magnificent animal of a man. Dark and massively muscular, his gigantic chest and limbs matted with wiry black hair, shiny with sweat and oil. Brutally handsome, with a bristling mustache and a broad smile that shows the gap between his two front teeth. His legs ride clear of the ground, bent back so that the tops of his feet rest against the boy's thighs. His big, loose balls are pooled in the small of the boy's back. His huge cock juts upward like a club. One arm reaches forward, clutching a fistful of blond hair. The other stretches back, holding a doubled leather belt. Rezi snaps it against the boy's ass, bellowing with laughter as the blond lurches forward, staggering under his weight.

Despite his muscular physique, the young blond looks absurdly small compared to the big Turk mounted on his back. His shoulders and arms strain beneath the burden, muscles standing out in stark relief. His head is wrenched back by the fist in his hair, his lean torso bent like a bow, thrusting his ass upward, showing off the sleek curve where his powerful buttocks flow into thick, sturdy thighs. Hairless and sleek, pale and glistening with sweat. Trembling beneath the weight, panting for breath, squealing and lurching forward as Rezi pops the belt against his naked ass. His stubby little pony-cock juts out bone-hard between his thighs, ridiculously small compared to the Turk's massive truncheon, bobbing ludicrously up and down, slapping up against his belly as he breaks into a trot.

Rezi drives him until they reach the wall. More slaps from the belt, and the boy awkwardly turns about, the top-heavy load shifting wildly on his back, threatening to capsize. Ahmed manages a sleepy laugh.

Rezi frowns at the boy's clumsiness. He twists his hair and barks a command in Turkish, leaning forward to slap the belt upward against his belly, landing a lucky shot that smacks the tip of the boy's penis. The blond whinnies and jerks forward, stamping across the carpet.

Benny smiles. "Rezi's not this rough with the Arab boys. It's the fair-haired numbers that bring out his mean streak. Should've seen the working over he gave the redhead last time he was here." He glances at the customer. The man's handsome features are strangely twisted, his eyes flashing with an intensity that makes Benny balk.

"His face," the man mutters. "I can't see his face."

"Sure. Sure, his face." Benny steps back and leans toward the speaker. He clears his throat. "Hey, boys. Having a good time?"

The Turks seem to welcome the intrusion. Abdul answers by grabbing his cock between two fingers and spanking it back and forth against his thighs. Rezi spins his head toward the mirror, surprised for an instant, then flashes a broad grin. He jerks on the boy's hair like a rein, pulling him to a sudden halt.

The blond gasps and turns his face away from the mirror. His body trembles on the verge of collapse. Perhaps from shame. Perhaps from exhaustion.

Beirut

Perhaps because he knows that something terrible is about to happen.

"Hey, don't let me interrupt." Benny tries to make his voice light and playful, but the strain comes through. The customer is getting on his nerves. "Got a guy out here who likes 'em blond and hunky. Wants a good look at the kid's face."

Rezi nods. He lowers his feet to the ground and slides backward, over the boy's ass and off, into a crouch. He tightens his grip on the boy's hair, pulling him back until his hands clear the carpet. Rezi tilts back on the balls of his feet, aiming his cock between the lashed and sweaty buttocks. Then he springs forward and up, straightening his legs. With a single thrust, he spears the boy to the hilt and stands upright.

The maneuver is a spectacle of raw strength, brought off with a kind of animal grace, as effortless as spearing a piece of meat on a fork. Except that this piece of meat is alive.

The boy goes rigid, paralyzed by the sudden, total penetration. Hands reaching back to claw at Rezi's hips. Head wrenched back, mouth open in a silent scream. Toes extended, feet paddling the air—Rezi's cock lifts him clear off the floor.

Rezi turns toward the mirror, displaying the nude, twitching body impaled on his cock, like a trophy mounted on his dick. Face pulled back, hands clutching Rezi's hips, the boy's body appears headless, armless, a sculptured mass of pale, agonized flesh suspended in midair and framed by the dark brawn of Rezi's body. The boy is sleek and hairless, denuded even between his legs. His chest breaks out in a sudden drenching sweat, running in a liquid sheet across the smooth slabs of muscle, collecting at the tips of his huge, obscenely bloated nipples.

Rezi cock-walks him toward the mirror, thrusting savagely with his hips. The boy suddenly comes alive. Skewered on the big cock, squealing and grunting and dancing like a puppet. His big, meaty pecs flop up and down. His stubby little cock slaps back and forth between his belly and thighs. Like a spastic walking on water, toes barely grazing the floor, driven forward by the cock up his ass.

They reach the mirror. Rezi grabs the boy's hips and hoists him up, clear off the cock. He bends at the knees and leans back, making his hips into a cradle, then lowers the boy onto the greasy pole of his cock. The boy sits on it in midair, hips tilted forward, back arched, legs dangling on either side of Rezi's steely thighs. Rezi is a show-off, making sure the men beyond the mirror have a clear view of the boy's hole, and the big cock stuffed inside.

He slides his hands up the boy's torso, cupping his breasts from behind. Squeezing the fleshy slabs between his forefingers and thumbs, making the big nipples pop out, wagging them at the mirror. Grinding his hips, making the boy's cock rotate in a jagged ellipse. Reaching down to give it a quick one-two slap with his open palms before reaching back to squeeze the boy's tits.

He pinches the nipples between his fingernails, tugging at the swollen buds as if he were trying to pluck them from the boy's chest. He clamps them between his fingertips, squeezing and pulling at the tips, milking him like a woman. Fucking him like a woman, while the others watch. Letting them all see what it means to be a toy for a man with a big dick and a cruel imagination. The boy groans and writhes, his head thrown back on Rezi's big shoulder.

"His face." The customer hisses through gritted teeth. "I still can't see his face."

Beirut

Benny gives a start, so fascinated by the spectacle beyond the glass that he's almost forgotten the reason. If he weren't in the middle of a deal, he'd be tempted to join in the fun himself. Nobody knows how to show off a hot piece of boycunt like Rezi ... except Vince Zorio, of course. It was Vince who found the blond in the first place. Vince who had the boy's pubic hair permanently removed; Vince who paid to have the silicone injected into his nipples. Vince who trained the boy how to open wide and drool from both ends at the mere sight of another man's cock.

Benny leans toward the speaker. His voice is hoarse and throaty. "C'mon Rezi. We already know you got the dick of death. Now show us the cocksucker's face."

Rezi flashes a cocky grin. Rezi likes to tease. He grabs a fistful of the boy's hair and thrusts his head toward the mirror.

The boy's forehead strikes the glass with a thump. Benny jerks back in alarm, but the customer steps closer, until his face and the boy's are only inches apart. The boy's nose and cheek are mashed flat against the glass. Jaw slack, mouth open and dribbling. Forehead beaded with sweat, plastered with stray tendrils of hair. His long blond lashes flutter; his blue eyes are glazed and staring. Humiliated and utterly helpless. No other sight on earth as beautiful—the face of a handsome boy with a really big one up his butt.

Benny gawks, as spellbound as the customer. Then he comes to his senses. He closes the curtains with a flourish. The customer is hooked, no doubt about it. Time to close the deal. Benny's eyes light up with dollar signs.

The customer stands stock-still, staring into the

darkness of the drapes, listening to the muffled noises that come from the cubicle beyond—a sudden volley of slapping, barking laughter and a high girlish shriek.

"So. What do you think? About as blond as they come. But hardly fresh."

"I want him."

"Maybe tomorrow, huh? The Turks have already been working him over for hours, and Rezi looks like he's just getting warmed up."

"Tonight. I won't be here tomorrow."

"Sure. Have to be late, though." An idea pops into Benny's head. "And there's an extra fee for sessions after midnight."

The customer turns and gives him a long, hard stare. "I'll be here at midnight, then. Have him cleaned up and ready for me." The look in his eyes is crazy again. Benny wonders about the bandage taped to the guy's temple. Maybe something's wrong with his head.

"Sure … By the way, the kid's name is David."

The man walks past him, giving no response. As if the boy's name doesn't interest him. Or as if he knew it already.

IV

David lies alone in the darkened cubicle. The lamp remains on—in Benny's place, the lights always stay on in the private rooms—but the switch is turned to the lowest wattage, bathing the room in a hazy dreamlike glow, amber and soft, like the last light of dusk in the dusty streets of Beirut.

Beirut

The room is hot and airless. David lies nude atop the soiled and rumpled sheet, glazed with sweat, too exhausted to move, every muscle stiff and aching. His eyes are closed, hovering between sleep and waking. His body seems as weightless as mist, defined only by the points that throb with a cloying erotic ache....

His throat and asshole, raw and swollen from Rezi's cock.

His nipples, throbbing in time with his heartbeat, too tender to touch.

His balls, heavy as lead, drawn up tight at the base of his cock, aching for relief.

His cock, jabbing stiff against his belly, sore and stinging at the tip. He longs to touch it, but he keeps his hands at his sides. Benny might be watching.

This is all he is: a mouth and an asshole, two nipples and a penis. The holes are for fucking. The rest are toys to be played with and tormented, pinched and whipped by the men who fuck him.

Vince Zorio did this to him. David did it to himself, in payment for the life he took from Sergeant Richter. If the sergeant could see him now—see what's become of the all-American kid who swore he'd never suck cock, who said he'd kill any man who tried to get a stiff one up his ass ...

His mind flashes back to the murder in the sleazy bar called Chez Fez, to the instant when the heavy bottle connected with Richter's skull and suddenly the whole world was awash in a sea of blood and wine. To the miserable weeks on the run, hunted and helpless in Beirut. Alone, speaking no Arabic or French, his wallet growing thinner by the day; saving the little money he had by eating scraps from refuse piles, counting himself lucky when he could steal an orange from the open bazaars, sleeping in the rubble, dodging the bands of guerrillas who patrol the streets at night. Waking every morning in the cool hours just before dawn, bathed in cold sweat and trembling from the nightmare memory of Sergeant Richter's face at the instant the bottle struck his temple.

The meeting with Abdul the forger made him realize just how desperate he was. The cash in his wallet counted for nothing. He had nothing to barter with, except the one thing he refused to give up. The thing Sergeant Richter died trying to take ...

David had been on the verge of giving himself up. Then, like a guardian angel from hell, Vince Zorio entered the picture. Zorio, who walked the dangerous streets of Beirut as if he owned them. Who said he could get David out of this mess, away from Beirut, alive and free. For a price.

David's eyelids flutter. Dreaming or awake, he can see it clearly before his face. Vince Zorio's cock. Sleek and massive, obscenely beautiful. Thick as a forearm, smooth as satin, laced with veins. Perpetually erect, constantly demanding satisfaction. The cock that took his cherry. The cock that turned his mouth into a cunt. The cock that turned his ass into a pussy.

Pussyboy. That's what Vince started calling him. For good reason.

Vince had only to enter the room, to flash his cocksure grin and grope himself casually, and David was reduced to nothing more than two holes at either end of his body; two cunts, warm and slick inside, both aching for the terrible pleasure that only Vince could give him. Desperate to please, willing to do anything the big man demanded.

And once Vince had him hooked, Vince never gave it for free. David had to beg for it. David had to crawl naked on his hands and knees, whimpering and pleading for Vince to fuck him. Even Rezi is a pale

Beirut

substitute. If God himself had a cock, it would be the cock that hangs between Vince Zorio's legs.

Step by step, Zorio has changed him beyond recognition. Twisting David's body inside out, rearranging it to please himself. Turning David's asshole into a mouth, a drooling, hungry hole kissing, sucking, swallowing cock. Making his mouth into an asshole, fucking it with long, hard, relentless strokes. Twisting his nipples into little cocks, standing up erect to be milked between the man's forefingers and thumbs, working them till David can almost come through his nipples. Turning his cock into a toy, a whipping post, a tender stalk with an overgrown nipple at the tip to be nibbled and pinched.

When Zorio took him to the specialist to make the permanent changes—denuding the hair from his body, injecting the silicone into his nipples—David allowed it with hardly a whimper of protest.

Still, it was never enough. The price is steep for the things that David needs: phony papers, safe housing, transport across international borders, petty bribes to a dozen bureaucrats along the way. Escape becomes more dangerous, and more costly, every day. Beirut slips deeper into chaos hour by hour. The marines are still looking for him. So are the local police. And any one of a dozen terrorist groups would be delighted to capture an AWOL American marine, for fun or profit.

Zorio has all the right connections. Zorio can get him out of Beirut in one piece. Zorio can even arrange a new identity for him back in the States. But Vince Zorio never takes on charity cases. David has to earn the money. That was how he ended up working at Benny's place.

"How long?" he asked, after the audition with Benny, as Zorio was getting ready to leave.

Vince shrugged. *"A year. Maybe less. Depends on how many clients you can handle in an average week. Benny takes most of the cut. Only fair. He's giving you room and board—plus all the dick a cocksucker like you ever dreamed of. Besides, he's taking a big risk just having you here.*

"The rest of your income goes to me. Once I collect my cut, we'll start a little account toward getting you home. Did I say a year? Maybe two. Jesus, stop sniveling, pussyboy. You can do hard time, or you can do easy time. Relax. Enjoy it. Now open wide and say good-bye to daddy's dick. Won't be seeing you for a while. That's it ... all the way down your throat...."

David has been here for seven weeks, but it might have been seven months, or seven years. Time stands still at Benny's place. There is no day or night in the little basement cubicles, only twilight. Clients come from all over the world, Old rich and new rich and commoners on a splurge, men with a craving for the special services only Benny's boys can provide. The customers arrive at all hours, one after another, a constant parade of cocks to stuff David's ass and cram his throat.

They make him work hard for the money. Once upon a time, David's surly good looks and muscular build intimidated other men. One look at him now, standing nude and submissive with his hands behind his back, and the customers know they can do whatever they please. A boy with a hairless crotch and nipples like that couldn't have any shame. A boy like that couldn't say no to anything.

If the sergeant could only see him now ...

David is awakened by a hard poke in the ribs.

"Rise and shine, cocksucker. Almost midnight. You got company coming." Benny pokes him again, using the sawed-off handle of a toilet plunger, his favorite tool for keeping his boys in line. Groggy with sleep, David rolls over, turning his back to the man. Benny gooses him with the wooden pole, poking it rudely between his cheeks. David gives a yelp and tumbles off the low bed, falling face down on the floor.

"I said, rise and shine. On your feet. *Now!*"

David staggers up. Benny helps him by grabbing a fistful of hair, then wakes him up with a few slaps across the face.

"That's better. Bright-eyed and bushy-tailed." Benny laughs. David has never known an uglier sound.

"Like I said, you got a client due any minute. You'll like him—big blond guy, American. Got all excited watching you do circus tricks for Rezi this afternoon. Told him you'd be a lousy fuck after the Turks, but it seems like he's on a limited schedule." Benny picks up a sack from the floor and empties it on the bed. David glances sidelong at the odds and ends, unable to make sense of them. "Guy had a few special requests. You know the kind, likes a boy to dress up special for him. And you know the rule at Benny's place—we'll do anything to please our clients. Right, cocksucker? So let's get started...."

David stands shivering and alone in the center of the room, waiting for the customer. What kind of man would want him this way? What kind of things will a man like that expect him to do?

The high-heeled pumps feel awkward on his feet, forcing him to stand on tiptoe, pitching his whole body forward in a lewd posture: legs rigid, ass high, abdomen slightly protruding. To compensate, he has to throw his shoulders back—not hard to do with his wrists handcuffed behind him.

The sheer silk stockings feel strange against his hairless legs, held up by the black garter around his thighs. The stockings themselves are almost transparent, turning shiny and opaque when the light strikes them, giving his sleek, muscular legs an almost metallic shimmer, a kind of see-through nudity more provocative than bare flesh.

Above the waist he wears nothing but a studded leather collar around his throat and a pair of shiny silver pasties with long black tassels attached to his oversized nipples. The bizarre accoutrements oddly accentuate the broad, deep-clefted muscularity of his shoulders and chest. His body shimmers with oil and sweat in the dull orange light.

His cock stands erect, almost numb, strangled at the base by a metal cockring two sizes too small. Benny had to whip his cock to get it soft enough to fit through the ring; even so, it was a bitch getting his balls to pop through. They snuggle up against the base of his erection, defying gravity like tiny helium-filled balloons. Like his cock, they look swollen to the point of bursting. The angry red color isn't completely natural; Benny applied a bit of rouge after he got the cockring on, then applied the same coloring to David's lips and cheeks.

The final touch is unseen: the eight-inch rubber dildo inserted up David's ass. The thing is like a pin up his spine. Together with the high heels and the handcuffs, it makes it almost impossible for him to move in anything resembling a normal fashion. Benny had a good laugh, forcing him to stagger and stumble in a circle about the tiny room, goading him on with the plunger handle.

Now Benny is gone, and David waits, standing stock-still in the center of the room, staring at his reflection in the mirror with fleeting glances, feeling hot and ashamed, dreading the long night ahead and wondering again about the man who wants him this way. The man who might be standing beyond the two-way mirror at this very instant, staring at him. David feels a sudden chill, a rippling of goose bumps across his oiled, sweat-misted flesh. He bites his lip and lowers his eyes to the floor.

He hears a sound from the hallway outside. His heart begins to race. The customer must be here at last. Then the sounds become clearer. Benny, shouting. Another man's voice, raised in anger—perhaps two other men.

Something is wrong. Very wrong.

There's a loud thump against the door, then the sound of a scuffle. An instant of silence, then a loud voice, speaking English with an American accent: "Open it up, goddammit! Now, you motherfucker!"

The key jangles in the lock. The door swings open. At the same instant, the two-way mirror explodes into the room, shattered into a million fragments.

Two of them. Two U.S. Marines. MPs in uniform. One stands in the doorway, his firearm drawn; Benny cowers behind him. The other stands where the mirror used to be, knocking away the last bits of glass with his rifle butt.

For a moment they stare at him, expressionless, slowly looking him up and down. Then they stare at each other. David blushes bright red to match the rouge on his cheeks. His heart beats faster still—so fast it feels like it might explode in his chest. His head goes dizzy. For a moment the MPs vanish, obscured by the oily spots before his eyes.

Their voices are muffled, as if his ears were stuffed with cotton:

"Damn! The sergeant was right on the money."

"Just like he told us—the mirror, the room. The way he's dressed. Jesus..."

"Think we oughta let him change—"

"No. We take him in just like he is. That was the arrangement."

"Except we'll need something to put over him in the street. Tell the fat guy to get something—some kind of overcoat..."

The next half-hour is all a nightmare, the reality reaching his mind only in splintered fragments. Benny yelling and blustering—one of the MPs punching him in the belly with the butt of his rifle. A moth-eaten overcoat thrown about David's shoulders, and the marines hustling him down the hallway, up the stairs, past rooms echoing with the sounds of sex after midnight—the slap of flesh against flesh, the crack of leather on skin, squeals, whimpers, sighs, moans—and finally, suddenly, into the moonlit street.

A third MP waits in the jeep, with the engine running. The jeep is the biggest shock of all. He hasn't seen one in so long—the memories ... Only in this instant does he comprehend what's happened. The MPs are taking him in. David is being arrested. Captured. All the months of being on the lam, all the things he's done for Vince and for Benny—all of it comes to nothing.

"Hey, Smitty."

"Yeah?"

"Didn't you forget something?"

"Oh, right." The MP next to him pulls out a big handkerchief, folds it, ties it like a blindfold over David's eyes.

They drive for only a few minutes; then the jeep comes to a full stop. The driver cuts the engine. The marine encampment is miles from Benny's place;

Beirut

they can't possibly be there yet. Or perhaps David's sense of time is askew from shock and sightlessness.

They hustle him out of the jeep, down a cobblestone walkway. David staggers behind the blindfold, trips in his heels. The dildo is like a spike up his ass. The men snigger and grab his arms, dragging him along. A door opens and shuts. Carpet beneath his feet. They step into a creaky elevator and ascend. Two stories, maybe three—they step into a hallway, then through another door.

David senses another presence in the room. The MPs push him forward, pulling the coat from his shoulders. He feels utterly naked and defenseless. The numbness between his legs tells him his cock is still erect, kept that way by the strangling metal ring. His skin prickles with a mixture of shame and dread.

"Here he is, Sarge. We found him, just like you said we would. Smitty, what time is it?"

"0100 hours, sir."

"Right. Look, Sarge, we can kill a few hours, say the arrest took more time than we thought. But no more than two hours. That's all I can give you. After that, I've got to get the prisoner back to HQ to start the paperwork. Two hours, okay?"

"Good enough. I've got an early-bird flight to Tel Aviv, anyway."

The unseen sergeant's voice is deep and flat, with a genteel Southern polish. Without quite knowing why, the sound of it does something strange to David, making him shiver even harder, making him blush a deeper, hotter red.

"Fair enough, Sarge. Shit, I figure you ought to have a crack at the little weasel—after what happened and all. Come on, Smitty, let's hightail it out of here for a couple of hours. Back at 0300, Sarge. Until then, whatever happens between you and the prisoner is strictly on the QT. The little faggot's all yours."

Someone tugs at the tassel hanging from one of David's nipples. Laughter. The door opens. Two sets of footsteps depart. The door slams shut.

David can feel the man approaching. He flinches at his touch—the calloused fingers brush his face and undo the blindfold. The cloth drops away. David blinks, dazzled for an instant by the dim candlelight that illuminates the room. A squalid little hotel room, four bare walls and a ratty bed, like a thousand other rooms in Beirut.

The first thing he sees is the man's back, walking away from him, clutching the blindfold in one fist. A big man, broad shouldered, the bulging muscles of his back clearly defined against the starched fabric of his uniform shirt. Blond, with his hair cut in a classic U.S. Marine Corps high-and-tight; his ears and the back of his neck are red from the sun. The man stands still for a long moment, then turns on his heel.

The candlelight casts deep shadows across his face, bathing his cheekbones and forehead with a ruddy glow. But even in the dimness there can be no doubt. David would know the face in his sleep—sleep is where he most often sees it, haunting his nightmares. A dead man's face. A demon from hell. The big-jawed, all-American, movie-star handsome face of Sergeant Richter, who died in an off-limits cafe called Chez Fez when a wine bottle smashed his skull.

David should know. David killed him.

"What's the matter, Private Patowski? Cat got your tongue?"

The ghost can speak. David is struck dumb. He opens his mouth—nothing that comes out would sur-

Beirut

prise him: a scream, a curse, a cry for help. But the only sound that emerges is a hoarse, ragged exhalation of shock.

The sergeant steps toward him, holding his trademark riding crop, tapping it against his boot. The sergeant always was a Virginia gentleman at heart, with old money and old-school connections. Even in Beirut he found the opportunity to go riding on Saturdays.

He raises the crop in the air and brings it down with a whoosh, stinging-hard against the tip of David's quivering penis.

David finally finds his voice. He howls and staggers backward. His heels catch in the carpet. He falls forward on his knees.

Richter steps closer. "What's the matter, Patowski? Maybe you thought I was dead? Just a scar." He reaches up absently and caresses the three-inch discoloration that mars his forehead and interrupts his hairline. "Take more than a little weenie like you to put me out of business."

David shakes his head. The last few months have taught him the difference between nightmare and cold reality. Richter is no hallucination. The sergeant is real, here, now, in this room. Which means he never died. Which means that everything David has done since the incident at Chez Fez has been utterly meaningless. Assaulting a superior officer would have landed him in hot water—or perhaps not, given the circumstances. Richter was only unconscious, not dead—there was no reason to flee. And no need for the annihilating guilt of the past months, the terror that's haunted him every hour, awake or sleeping. His arrangements with Zorio, his servitude at Benny's, the endless punishments he's inflicted on himself—all meaningless and unnecessary. Because Richter is alive.

And more than meaningless—because, despite his protests and resistance, despite the bottle he used against the man's skull at Chez Fez—the truth is that David wanted Sergeant Richter's cock all along.

"Look at you." Richter towers above him. A bottle of whiskey in one hand, the riding crop in the other. "Look at yourself, faggot. Slutboy. Scumbag. That dildo feel good up your cunt? Huh? Feel all sexy in your silk stockings? Why don't you shake your tassels for me—see if you can get me hot."

Richter steps closer, until David's nose is only inches from the sergeant's crotch. The bulge is unmistakable. Hung like a horse—everybody knows that, common gossip in the whole platoon.

"This is how they'll all see you when the MPs bring you in." Richter laughs and takes a swig from the bottle. "Just like this. Damn, they are gonna throw the book at you, cocksucker. After they finish hooting. No mercy for a piece of trash like you. A U.S. Marine working like a common whore at a Beirut brothel, letting every camel jockey from here to Teheran shoot a load up his butt. Shit, once they stop laughing, the brass is gonna bury you so deep you'll never see daylight. And I don't think they'll be much impressed by your excuses. Saying you deserted the marines because your sarge made a pass at you—it just ain't gonna wash."

Richter steps even closer. His crotch brushes against David's lips. His voice is a whisper. "Know what it's like in a marine prison barracks? Got any idea? What do you think's gonna happen when you show up, with your pretty blond hair and your smooth, pretty muscles—not to mention your reputation. And how about the first time they see you naked in the showers? Not a hair between your legs, and those big, puffed-up nipples. Sure hope you've

Beirut

changed your mind about sucking cock, boy. I got a feeling that's gonna be just about your only pastime for the next five or ten years."

Richter's crotch is pressed flush against David's face. The starched fabric is stiff and scratchy against his lips. He can feel the heat of the man's sex through the cloth. He can smell its musk.

Richter reaches down and undoes the clasp of his belt. He undoes his pants and peels back the right-hand panel. The zipper descends with a faint slithering noise.

David draws back and takes a shuddering breath. He can see the outline clearly through Richter's boxer shorts. The big cock gives a jerk and tumbles out of the fly. The head butts against his mouth, squirting a dollop of semen onto his lips.

David stares at it, cross-eyed. A big, blond cock, plump and meaty, just beginning to stiffen. He narrows his eyes until the room disappears, and even the cock is a hazy blur. He parts his lips. Opens wide.

And smashes sideways onto the floor, his face stinging and his ears ringing from the force of Richter's slap.

"Get back up on your knees, bitch."

David rolls dizzily onto his knees and manages to lift himself upright. He swings about and accidentally slaps his cheek against Richter's cock. The contact burns his flesh. He flinches back and squints. The fleshy tube is firmer now, projecting at a pliant angle from the sergeant's open fly. Somewhere above, Richter is unbuttoning his shirt, pulling the tails from his pants, shrugging it from his shoulders.

David's mouth opens of its own accord. He leans forward. His lips make contact with the smooth, shiny crown of Richter's cock. His tongue touches the moist tip. He pushes his mouth onto the pole. The flesh is marvelously warm and sleek.

A slap and a pop, a squeal and a muffled crash, all in an instant. David lies crumpled on the floor again, his head spinning. Richter has a strong right arm.

And heavy boots. He gives David a sharp kick in the ribs. "Back up on your knees. Right now, faggot."

David staggers up, his temples throbbing, his face aflame. Richter's cock is waiting for him. Bigger than before. Thicker. Standing up at a sharp angle from his pants, the first three inches glistening with a shiny coat of spit.

David leans toward it, lips parted. Close enough to kiss—the odor overwhelms him. At the last instant he flinches and rolls his eyes up.

Richter towers above him, stripped to the waist. Everything a marine should be. Blond. Muscular. Broad shouldered and big chested, with a light dusting of gold across his hard, square pectorals. Hands on his hips, standing cock-proud with a forearm of flesh jutting sleek and naked from his open pants. The same cock he offered to David long ago. The cock that would have claimed his cherry, if David had only allowed it.

David leans toward it, feeling its warmth against his face, feeling a gnawing hunger in his belly and a strange emptiness in his throat. "Please. Please let me suck it...."

His mouth makes contact. He swallows half the pole, stretching his lips around the width. Richter slaps him to the ground.

Over and over. Richter allows him to suck it, but only for an instant. Richter slaps him down. Richter forces him back up to his knees, then brandishes the thing in his face, taunting him with it, bobbing it up and down, slapping it like a blackjack against his

Beirut

face. The cock seems to grow bigger and stiffer each time.

David begs. David impales his mouth on the big cock. Richter slaps him to the ground.

Until the sergeant abruptly grabs him by a fistful of hair and pulls him staggering to his feet, spins him around and shoves him against the wall.

"Ass in the air, faggot."

David obeys. Instantly. Without question. He spreads his legs and bends deep, pushing his cheeks up and open, bringing his face almost to the ground, striving to keep his balance with his hands cuffed behind him.

Richter seizes the butt of the dildo and pulls it out with a pop. David gasps. The musty air feels warm and humid against his exposed hole. The sudden emptiness is like a wound. The craving moves instantly from his mouth to his ass.

Richter grabs his belt buckle. The black leather slithers out of the belt loops. He wraps it twice around his fist.

"Seems to me, Private Patowski, that my memory must be a bit hazy. Seems to me I recall a little speech you gave me one night at Chez Fez. You recall that night, private?"

The belt slashes through the air. David screeches. *"Yes, sir!"*

"Like I say, maybe my memory's off. Never been quite the same since a little accident I had. Some stupid shit hit me in the head with a wine bottle."

"Sir—please, sir—" For some reason, David starts to cry.

The belt whooshes through the air. Leather strikes naked flesh with a sweaty crack. "Shut up, private. Speak when you're spoken to. Now help me refresh my memory. What exactly was it you said to me that night? Before you swung the bottle at me?"

"Please, sergeant, I don't remember—"

The belt swings down and connects with a sound like a rifle shot.

"Stop blubbering, faggot. Repeat the words you spoke to me that night. Do it now."

"Please, sir, I said—I said—"

A whoosh. A crack. A squeal.

"I'm not a cocksucker!" David shouts the words. The belt comes down. *"I'm not a pussy!"* Richter swings the belt. *"I am not a cocksucking faggot, Sir!"*

Richter drops the belt. Two steps and the head of his cock is flush against the strap-marked opening of David's hole. He lays his hands on David's cheeks, grabs two fistfuls of piping hot flesh and squeezes hard.

David hisses through his tears. Richter's cock prods his asshole. In his mind's eye he can see it, bloated to maximum erection, glossy with spit, poking at the entrance to the his bowels.

"Now say the truth," Richter whispers. "Say it. Tell me what you want, faggot."

David grits his teeth. The hole between his legs yawns open, enormous and empty, needing a man to fill it up.

"Go ahead, queerboy. Cocksucker. Marine pussy. Tell the sergeant what you want."

David shouts the words, tears streaming down his face. *"Fuck me! Oh, please, Sir! Please, for God's sake, fuck me, Sarge!"*

Richter swings his hips back an inch, then plows forward, driving his cock all the way to the balls in David's guts.

Promptly at 0300 hours, there's a sharp rapping on the door.

Beirut

Richter is checking his appearance in the small shaving mirror that hangs above the rusty sink. "Just a minute," he calls over his shoulder. He finishes knotting his tie, straightens it with a tug, then turns about.

The bed is a shambles. At some point, it actually broke in two. The mattress lies akilter in its frame, collapsed on one side with broken slats beneath. The pillows are scattered on the floor. The sweat-stained sheets are rumpled and twisted into knots.

On the floor in front of the bed, David kneels like a Moslem facing Mecca—ass up, feet pressed together, face against the floor, hands cuffed in the small of his back. His buttocks are covered with angry red marks. Handprints. Belt marks. Deeper welts inflicted by Richter's crop. A white, opalescent fluid streams from his nostrils and the corner of his mouth, forming a pool on the floor. The same liquid oozes from his raw, chafed sphincter, trickling down the insides of his thighs—Richter's semen, leaking from every hole in his body.

A man like Richter can shoot a lot of come in two hours. In two hours a man like Richter can do a lot to a boy like David, especially when the boy is nude and handcuffed and does nothing to resist.

Richter walks to the bed. He ruffles through the sheets and finds the dildo. Without ceremony, he bends down and shoves it into David's rectum. The hole is so worn and stretched that the hourglass base of the dildo won't catch; it oozes out of David's ass with a fart and falls to the floor with a thud.

Richter scowls and gives a snort of disgust. He steps behind David and gives him a hard kick in the ass, punching the toe of his boot square against the boy's gaping sphincter. David responds with a whimpering grunt. More semen leaks from his holes.

"So long, sucker. See you at the court-martial."

Richter plucks his cap from the bedstead, straightens it across his brow, opens the door.

The MPs, all three of them, are waiting in the hall. Richter smiles and casually salutes. "The prisoner is all yours, gentlemen."

The MPs salute in return, then file into the room without a word. The one called Smitty closes the door behind them.

Richter steps toward the elevator, then pauses for a moment and inclines his ear toward the door. From within he can hear sounds of slapping, punching, a hoarse grunt followed by a squeal. The sounds cease for a moment, then continue again, louder.

Just as he thought. The MPs are in no hurry. The 0300 cutoff was so they could get their own crack at the prisoner. David probably won't arrive at HQ for another four hours.

Just as well. Richter would have liked having those extra hours for himself. But he's gotten his licks in; let the MPs have their fun. A little reward for a job well done.

Richter steps into the elevator and pulls the grille shut. The cage lurches and begins its descent. Even above the hum of the old motor he can hear David's high, shrill whimper, desperately panting and squealing: *Fuck me! Fuck me! Fuck me, sir!*

Or perhaps the voice comes only from his imagination, an echo of sweet memory.

KIP

» THE HIT «

The hotel waiter is surprisingly young. And blond. And very, very nervous, all dressed up in his blue monkey suit and black bow tie. Earlier, watching him wheel the breakfast cart into the suite, Vince wondered what the kid would look like naked.

The waiter is pouring his coffee now, holding the china saucer and cup in one hand and the small porcelain pitcher in the other—jangling the cup against the saucer, splattering a few drops onto the deep green spread that covers the serving cart. The kid's lips move soundlessly, forming a curse and then suppressing it. He glances quickly at Vince, then at the hair-matted cleft of muscle exposed between the flaps of Vince's robe, then quickly away. The more nervous he gets, the cuter he looks.

Vince takes a drag off his cigarette and exhales the smoke through his nostrils with an audible rush, letting the kid know he's impatient for the coffee. He spreads his legs beneath the cart and leans back in his chair, letting the robe open another inch or two across his chest. The heavy silk drags sensuously over his thighs, and Vince feels the stirrings of an erection. He bought the robe the week before, during a job in Kansas City, at a fancy high-priced men's shop. In his line of work, at the age of thirty-one, Vincent Zorio can afford to treat himself to the very best.

"You always take this long, kid?" Vince mutters the words softly, but the boy jerks and almost loses the cup.

"No, sir." The kid looks him in the eye for an instant and swallows nervously. He holds out the cup. It jangles in his hand. "Your coffee, sir?"

"Yeah, my coffee. If you're finished spilling it all over the tablecloth."

"I'm sorry, sir. If—"

"Just set it down on the cart."

"Will there be anything else, sir? I mean, if you'll just sign the check ..."

"Sure." A silver pen lies beside the green-bordered slip of paper, both stamped with the hotel's crest. Vince studies the check for a long moment, feeling the kid's nervousness, feeling his cock growing longer, unfurling warm and thick against the inside of his thigh.

"Is something wrong, sir?"

Vince signs the check and sits back in the chair, holding the pen between his thumb and forefinger, studying it.

"How old are you, kid?"

"Sir?"

"I said; How old are you?"

"Nineteen. Almost twenty."

"Kinda young to be working this job, in a hotel

like this. I'd figure you for a bellboy maybe. Or a maid's helper."

Vince glances up. The kid is actually blushing. He'll be biting his lip next. Looking blonder and cuter than ever.

"I've been at this job almost two years, sir, ever since I got out of school. I've never really had any complaints—"

"Shit, they hired you right out of high school? You must have connections."

The kid looks down and shrugs. The uniform jacket stretches tight across his chest. His body is lean and broad shouldered, slim hipped, with intimations of smooth muscle inside his tight blue uniform. "Well, yeah, I guess. My uncle Max is head chef—"

"Yeah, figures. What's your name?"

"Kip."

Vince nods. He always likes to know a kid's name before he dicks him. And, in the last two minutes Vince has made up his mind that the least he'll be getting from cute little Kip is a long and very thorough blowjob.

Vince puts the pen down beside the check. "I guess you expect a tip." He pushes his chair back and stands, walks to the dresser and returns with his wallet. His cock pushes up against the heavy silk, tenting the robe and swaying as he walks. He catches the boy staring, then looking away. Blushing darker than before.

Vince sits. "You have breakfast this morning, Kip?" The kid looks puzzled. "Uncle Max feed you down in the kitchen? Maybe a big juicy sausage, with a couple of eggs?" Kip flinches; Vince has aimed at a nerve and struck it, dead center. He pulls out a fifty and lays it on the cart beside the check. "Still hungry?"

The boy stares at the fifty, uncertain. As green as they come. Vince likes that. He picks up his fork, spears one of the fat link sausages on the gold-rimmed china plate, watches the grease erupt. He says the words again: "You still hungry, Kip? Maybe Uncle Max didn't feed you enough sausage this morning."

The kid looks him straight in the eye. Blushing. Breathing unevenly. Swallowing.

"Push this cart out of the way."

The boy moves to obey automatically. Vince loosens the sash around his waist and pushes aside the flaps of his robe. The boy turns back and sucks in his breath.

Vincent Zorio is a big man. Massive shoulders and chest, huge biceps and thighs, hard muscle without a trace of fat. A big booming voice, intimidating even when he speaks softly. Extra-large feet and hands—a strangler's hands, or a butcher's, meaty and thick. And a cock to match. It snakes beyond the edge of the chair, heavy and thick, balanced atop the plump cushion of his testicles.

Vince sits back in the chair, sliding his hips forward, spreading his thighs apart. He narrows his eyes. His dick grows into a fat, swollen truncheon of meat, curving outward and up, pointing straight at the boy's face. Kip's eyes are lowered, his lips parted. No longer looking Vince in the face, but staring at the cock. Waiting to be told.

"Go ahead, Kip. Put your mouth on it."

Kip fumbles toward him. Drops to his knees. Stares at the cock for a long moment. Then he looks up at Vince's chest, and his eyes glaze.

Vince smiles. *Christ, you got a great body, mister ... that's what the last kid told him, the cute little brunet with the bubble butt back in Kansas City. But

Kip

that one Vince picked up on the street—a common little gutter whore, shameless with his mouth. Little Kip is a different story. With Kip, Vince will do all the talking.

Kip's eyes return to the cock. He stares. His chest rises and falls inside the tight blue jacket. He lets out a little moan, then closes his eyes and opens wide, moving forward blindly to take it in his mouth.

Vince butts the palm of his hand against the kid's forehead. "Not so fast, cocksucker." He squeezes his cock at the base and aims it at Kip's mouth, hunching forward until he can feel the boy's warm breath on his dick. Kip stares at it, cross-eyed. "First you kiss it. You look me straight in the eye like a good little cocksucker, and you give my dick a nice, sloppy kiss."

Kip looks up. Eyes hungry, pleading. He seems to hesitate, then presses his lips against the fat bulb of flesh.

The contact electrifies him. Kip shudders and his face burns bright red. The muscles in his neck twist and contract. His Adam's apple twitches; the bow tie does a dance. Vince settles even deeper into the chair. It is all decided now.

"Yeah, kid," Vince croons, "Now wrap your lips around the head and give my dick a deep, wet French kiss.

Vince stares at the connection: the long, thick shaft leading like a tube into the boy's mouth, the wide-open lips stretched taut around the crown, the boy's hollowed cheeks and glittering eyes staring wildly back at him. His scrutiny is so blatant that Kip finally shuts his eyes tight, embarrassed; but his tongue never stops squirming against the swollen knob of flesh.

Vince studies the boy attached to the end of his dick. Kip is on all fours, his butt sticking up behind him, pressing firm and round against the seat of his pants. Both hands grip the thick cream-colored carpet—no move to touch himself. Everything centers on his mouth and the knob inside it, and the nine-tenths of Vince's cock still waiting to be sucked. A natural submissive. Vince knows the type, inside and out. Cock-hungry boy. Born to be dicked. Vince sized him up the moment he walked in the door, and Vince is never wrong.

"Good boy." He pats Kip's hollowed cheek, at first gently, then harder, almost slapping him. "Good little cocksucker." Vince grabs a fistful of silky blond hair. "Now we feed you the whole thing." Kip's face flashes alarm, and he grunts in protest—and then the grunt turns to a gurgle as his throat is filled with Vince's cock.

Kip heaves and chokes, spewing a mass of saliva into the pubic hair against his lips. He struggles to pull his head off the cock, but Vince holds him tight—then jerks the boy's head back, wrenching the cock from his mouth. It snaps against Vince's belly, then ricochets meaty and wet against the boy's stunned face.

Vince's eyes are heavy-lidded with lust. He purses his lips. "Mmm. That felt good, cocksucker. Let's do it again."

Before Kip can react, Vince yanks him back onto the cock, spearing it all the way down his throat. Gagging him with it. Listening to him sputter, feeling him heave. Screwing Kip's face into the wiry pubic thatch and savoring the deep-throat convulsions. After a long moment, Vince jerks the boy's head back and empties his mouth again.

Kip's face is drawn into a long silent howl, like a deep-sea diver breaking surface and gasping for air. Vince grips his cock at the base and spanks his face

Kip

with it, keeping him off base and dizzy. Kip squeals and tries to say something—but then the cock is lodged deep in his throat again.

This is the way Vince likes it—dominating a kid with his dick. Force-feeding him. Bludgeoning his throat. Punishing him with it and watching him open wide for more. Vince rides the boy's face, holding him by both ears, grinding his head into his lap and screwing it like a cored melon. Yanking his meat out of the kid's mouth and spanking him with it. Rubbing it huge, wet, and slick all over his face, until Kip is drunk with cock.

Vince croons. Beneath him Kip whimpers, gasps, makes strange mewling sounds of desire. The kid is into it now, wanting it bad. Wanting to join in. He balances himself awkwardly on one hand and gropes at the hardness cramped inside his pants. Vince kicks his hand away, and the boy submits, reaching instead with both hands to steady himself against the hard wooden legs of the chair while Vince begins a fresh volley of thrusts down his throat.

Suddenly Vince kicks him away, sending him sprawling against the floor. Kip looks up at him, confused and hurt. Then hungry again, staring up at the huge cock as Vince stands and steps toward him. Then abruptly alarmed, shrinking against the door as the big man looms over him. Vince towers like a giant above him—the broad muscles of his thighs foreshortened, the big cock thrusting upward from his groin, slick and bloated from fucking Kip's throat. His big balls are pulled up tight against the base of the shaft, silky smooth and as swollen as his cock.

Vince smirks. He pinches the base of his cock between his forefinger and thumb and spanks the air with it, watching the boy's eyes as they follow the beat. The kid is his now. He could pull him up off the floor, strip him, run his hands over that smooth, naked boyflesh—see what little Kip looks like bent over the bed naked with a big cock up his ass....

Vince glances at the clock on the dresser—a quarter to nine. Already running late. The best will have to wait.

Up," he growls, beckoning with his cock. "On your knees, kiddo." Kip scrambles to rise. Too slow. Vince grabs him by the hair and pulls his face to crotch level. Kip's eyes are closed, his mouth already open. A natural.

"Cocksucker," Vince whispers, hitting hard on the consonants. He pushes into the waiting hole—between the glistening lips, beyond the clenching sphincter. Deep in Kip's throat, his cock starts to twitch like a snake on hot asphalt.

Kip chokes, caught by surprise. Then his throat begins an automatic undulating caress around the cock, milking it as it empties itself into his belly. Vince throws his head back and growls, twisting Kip's face into his groin, burying his cock another few inches in the boy's neck. His hips shudder and convulse, and Kip's throat spasms in response.

After a long moment, the orgasm peaks, then slowly subsides. Vince keeps his cock lodged deep in the boy's throat, savoring the afterglow and the warm, clenching heat. Finally he pulls himself free.

Below him, Kip squats on folded knees, both hands pressed between his thighs, desperately kneading the bulge in his tight blue trousers. Vince smirks and reaches down, scooping the boy up by his armpits. He brushes Kip's hands away from his crotch. The boy moans in frustration. He clutches Kip's wrists, pins his arms to his sides, and runs his tongue over the boy's face—across cheeks slick with

Kip

saliva, over lips wet and shiny with semen. He covers the boy's mouth and kisses him—harsh, demanding, sucking Kip's breath away and then forcing it back into his lungs.

Vince breaks the kiss. He pushes Kip against the door and pats him roughly on the cheek, then turns and walks to the chair, stretching his arms above his head, belting his robe before he sits and draws the cart back in front of him.

Kip stands at the door, dazed, breathing hard, reaching up to wipe his mouth with the back of his hand.

Vince looks at him sharply. "Clear out, kid. Uncle Max'll be missing you down in the kitchen."

Kip hesitates, then turns and reaches for the doorknob.

"Hey, kid." Kip turns back, glancing guiltily at Vince for an instant before returning his gaze to the floor.

"Better take the check. And your tip."

Kip bites his lower lip and walks slowly to the cart. He reaches for the tray with trembling fingers, staring at the fifty on top. Vince catches him by the wrist, reaches for his wallet and adds a twenty.

Kip accepts the money in silence. He walks shakily to the door.

"Hey—cocksucker."

Kip freezes. He looks over his shoulder. Vince is sitting back in his chair, smoking a cigarette and smirking at him. "You take it up the ass, pussyboy?" Kip blushes. "Yeah, sure you do. What time you get off work?"

"I—" Kip clears his throat. His neck feels swollen and bruised inside. "Seven."

Vince nods. "Be here at eight sharp. That'll give you time to grab some dinner. Eat light. And don't bother to change—I like the little bow tie. Not that you'll be wearing your monkey suit for long." Vince takes a drag off his cigarette. "I wanna see what you look like naked."

Kip clears his throat again. "I—I don't know...."

"And keep your hands off your dick. Understand? You just keep that little boner tucked up and twitching inside your pants all day, and think about what I got waiting for you here between my legs."

Kip stares at the doorknob. He grips it tight to keep his hand from shaking. "I don't know," he whispers hoarsely. "I have to go now." Without looking back, he opens the door and slips away.

The coffee is cold, the food lukewarm. Vince doesn't mind. He wolfs down his breakfast in two minutes flat. A blowjob in the morning always makes him hungry.

After breakfast he dresses quickly, choosing his black suit and suede overcoat; the day is hardly chilly enough for it, but the bulk will help conceal the gun strapped across his shoulder. He checks himself in the mirror mounted above the dresser, and glances at the clock. Nine sharp. An instant later, he hears Battaglia's telltale knock at the locked door that joins the separate bedrooms of the suite.

It will all be over by five o'clock. Until then, he and Battaglia will be walking on glass every instant. The job is going to be a bitch. But once it's over, Vince will be twenty grand richer.

Besides, he has an evening with Kip to look forward to. There's always a chance that he's spooked the kid, but Vince remembers the look in Kip's eyes when the boy screwed up his face to kiss the fat knob of his cock. The way he opened his throat for it, like a holster to a gun. Action speaks louder than words, and a big dick speaks loudest of all to a cock-hungry

Kip

kid like Kip. There isn't a doubt in his mind that the boy will come knocking at his door exactly on time, blushing and biting his lip, looking blonder and cuter than ever.

Vince will have some surprises for him.

Ten till eight: Kip steps into the service elevator off the kitchen and presses the button for the fifteenth floor.

All day long, he has thought of Vince Zorio's cock, and nothing else. The way it filled his mouth. The way it stung his face when the man dredged it shiny and wet from his throat and beat him with it. The taste, overpowering and musky, when Vince packed it all the way home and started shooting.

Big. Big enough to choke him. Bigger than Uncle Max—and Max never uses his cock on Kip the way Vince did. Max never pushes him around, never calls him a cocksucker. Max is always happy to suck Kip off in return. Vince wouldn't even let him touch himself.

Kip has been with relatively few men, despite his looks and his eagerness. A couple of jocks used to let him suck them off in the locker room, but it never amounted to much. Kip is naturally timid about sex and embarrassed by the things he thinks about, naked and alone at night, beating his meat and imagining another man above him—always above, never beneath or beside. Shameful things—like the things Vince Zorio did to him.

Max was the first to fuck him. It was never said outright, but that was one of the conditions of the job: that Kip would do certain favors in return for Uncle Max's help. Kip seldom admits it to himself, but this is what turns him on most about sex with Max—the dirtiness of it, the way it makes him feel soiled and small.

Sometimes he wishes that Max would push harder. Usually it's nothing more than a hurried exchange of blowjobs, or a quick fuck in one of the vacant rooms. But when he lies naked with his fantasies, with his cock in his fist, Kip likes to imagine Max turning mean and ugly ... calling him names, ordering him around ... touching him in front of the other employees, letting them all know that he whores for his uncle. But Max will never be the man for that, and Kip is too shy to ever share his fantasies aloud.

Sometimes he has sex with guests at the hotel. They are always older. They always pay. As often as not, they simply want to suck him off. Kip gives them what they want, even though he wants it the other way around. He prefers the ones who want him to do the sucking. Best of all are the men who pay to fuck him. Kip never refuses, even if the man is old or ugly or fat. There is something intoxicating about pulling down his pants and bending over to let a stranger use him. They always rave about his beautiful ass....

But in two years of working at the hotel, two years of whoring for Max and the men passing through, Kip has never met a man like Vince Zorio. He first saw him the previous afternoon, checking into the hotel with another man, older and bigger and equally well dressed. Later, Kip sneaked a look at the register: Vincent Zorio, Leo Battaglia, Suite 1505, home addresses in New York. When the breakfast orders arrived that morning, he spotted Zorio's room number and took rounds for the fifteenth floor. It caused an argument with Walter, the headwaiter—the top floor always tipped the best. Max stepped in to settle it, and Walter was out of luck.

As soon as he entered the suite, Kip had gone weak in the knees. The sight of the man wearing nothing but his robe unnerved him; Vince Zorio was darkly handsome, with wavy black hair and strong, blunt features, and an impressive physique that had been obvious even in a business suit. And even before the man showed him his cock and told him to suck it, somehow Kip knew it would be a big one.

But there was something beyond the man's sheer physical appeal that made Kip turn jelly inside. The sex was like a dream, unreal and out of control, pulling Kip helplessly along; but the fascination went beyond even that. There was something dark inside Vincent Zorio, powerful and frightening. Kip had glimpsed it. He had responded to it; submitted to it; craved it—but exactly what it was escaped him, and he was not sure he wanted to know.

Somehow Kip managed to get through the day. Late in the afternoon there was an echo of excitement from the hotel lobby—a headline two inches tall on the front page of the evening paper, something about TWO EXECUTIVES SHOT TO DEATH in an office building only a few blocks away. But to Kip, everything was tedium. He worked in a haze, replaying the incident in Zorio's room over and over in his head. His cock stayed so hard inside his pants that it hurt, his balls felt swollen and full; but he did as the man had told him to do, and kept his hands away from the day-long ache between his legs....

Now, ascending in the elevator, Kip begins to feel loose and weak between his legs. Vince Zorio intends to fuck him. The man as much as told him so. Vince is going to fuck him, in his room, only minutes from now. Not a quickie, with Kip's pants pushed down around his ankles. *I wanna see what you look like naked*—that's what the man said. Vince is going to make Kip strip. Vince is going to fuck him naked.

The man will be rough—Kip knows that. Fucking his ass the way he fucked his face. It will hurt. It always hurts some, at first, even with smaller men. Kip wonders if Vince will let him touch himself while he's being fucked. It wouldn't hurt as bad that way; but it doesn't really matter. Kip liked it, somehow, the way the man denied him this morning, as if his own big cock was the only thing that mattered, as if Kip's cock wasn't worth the effort and didn't deserve to be touched.

Perhaps Vince will let Kip suck it before he fucks him with it. Or maybe the man will make him wait until afterwards, making him lick the big cock clean after it's been up his ass, calling him cocksucker and pussyboy and slapping his face. Maybe he will make Kip beg for it. Kip will beg. He will crawl on his hands and knees naked and beg for the privilege of sucking Vince Zorio's dick....

Five minutes to eight: Kip knocks at the door to suite 1505. His hands are sweaty. His mouth is dry. He listens to his heartbeat pounding in his throat while he waits for Vince to answer the door.

The doorknob turns; the door swings open. The first thing Kip notices is the the heavy shadow of stubble across Vince's jaw, then the smell of alcohol on his breath.

Vince gives him a cool smile and nods. "Come on in, kid."

Vince walks to the dresser. He still wears the black suit, but the collar of his shirt is undone, the thin black tie loosened around his neck. The room is lit softly. On the dresser stands an empty glass, and beside it a half-empty bottle of expensive bourbon.

Vince lights a cigarette. He reaches for the bourbon and pours himself a drink. He stares at Kip in the tall, wide mirror above the dresser. The cigarette hangs from the corner of his mouth.

Kip

"What are you waiting for, kid? I'm not paying to watch you model your monkey suit. Take it off."

Kip hesitates. With the other men there is usually a drink first, mention of money, some talk to feel him out. But Vince isn't like the others. That is what had brought him here, after all.

He reaches up to undo his tie.

"The bow tie stays," Vince says sharply. "Take off everything else."

Kip's fingers shake as he unbuttons his jacket and shrugs it off his shoulders. He takes off the stiffly starched white shirt, then peels off his T-shirt, wet with perspiration in the armpits. The refrigerated air is cool against his skin; his nipples turn to gooseflesh, but his face is burning hot.

The patent-leather shoes. The black nylon socks. Then his blue trousers, always hard to get out of. Max ordered them a size too small. Max likes them tight. Kip almost trips stepping out of them. He is naked now, except for a bow tie and black nylon briefs. He hesitates, suddenly self-conscious and uncertain.

"That's far enough," Vince says. He holds the glass of bourbon in one hand. The cigarette hangs from his lips. He stares at Kip in the mirror and motions with the glass. The ice cubes swirl and tinkle softly. "Turn around."

Kip turns and stands rigid. He can feel the man's eyes on his ass, burning hot. He hears the sound of Vince swallowing, then the clink of the glass being placed on the dresser; then Vince's breathing, close behind him.

"Well, well. You dress up special for the occasion—or do all you bellboys wear panties under your outfits?"

Kip flushes. His skin prickles in the cool air. His

briefs are sheer black nylon, skimpier than any bathing suit. They ride high in the back, digging into the crack of his ass and exposing the bottom curve of each cheek. In front they narrow to a snug little pouch that cramps his genitals even when they're soft. Max ordered a half-dozen in assorted colors from a mail-order outfit in Hollywood. The catalogue called it *The Cupcake Thong—for the young male beauty with his assets in the rear.*

"I asked you a question, Kip." Vince's breath is warm and moist in his ear, heavy with booze. "You always wear panties?"

Kip's voice is small and hoarse. "Yes."

"Umm. Cute." Vince cups his hand over one of the boy's firm buns, feeling the smoothness of the nylon against his palm and the even silkier flesh against his fingertips. He slides his middle finger under the hem, over the curve of Kip's ass and into the cleft. He strokes the tightly puckered hole, and Kip sighs in response. "Oh, kid, fucking your hole is gonna be a dream. Yeah. Now be a good little girl and take off your panties for me."

A trickle of sweat runs from Kip's armpit down the side of his chest. Vince is already taking him places he has never been, even in his fantasies. He slides the black panties over his hips and bends to peel them down his thighs.

Vince purses his lips. Sucks in his breath. The kid's ass is flawless. Smooth and white as ivory. Plump but firm, superbly shaped. A real bubble butt, perfect for screwing.

Kip stands, arms at his sides, eyes downcast. Vince slowly circles him, nodding approval. The boy's sturdy little cock stands straight up. The bow tie adds a sluttish touch, like a stripper's prop, flaunting his nudity.

Kip

"You work out, kid?"

Kip can hardly speak. "There's a gym in the basement. And a pool ..."

Vince nods. The kid's body is even better than he had hoped. Lean, muscular limbs, sharply defined under porcelain skin. A flat belly, gently ridged with muscle. Slender hips. A natural posture that pulls his broad shoulders up and keeps the small of his back arched stiffly, making his ass jut out hard and round behind him, lifting his pectorals up for display.

And it's the boy's pecs that Vince can't help staring at. The kid lifted weights to get a pair like that, did a lot of swimming. It shows—big, thick pectorals, pumped-up and round, glazed with a thin sheen of perspiration that makes them shine in the dimly lit room. So big they look lewdly out of place, top-heavy above the sinewy slenderness of his torso, extending a blatant, passive invitation to be cupped and fondled. Capping the smooth mounds are nipples an inch wide, standing out puffy and pink, ripe for plucking.

Vince likes big tits. On his women. On his boys. Twin handfuls of smooth, pliant muscle he can reach around and grab hold of when his cock is buried balls-deep in ass. Nipples he can pull on to make that ass do a grinding dance around his dick.

Vince takes a swig of bourbon. Then he takes an ice cube from the glass. Slowly, watching the boy's reaction, he touches it to the tip of each protruding nipple. Kip flinches and sucks in his breath. The icy contact makes his nipples crinkle and stiffen, erecting them into elongated little nubs of flesh. Vince toys casually with the effect, drawing a gasp from the boy each time he flicks the wedge of ice against the sensitive, swollen tips.

Kip is astonished at the sensation. His tits begin to

sting and burn. He closes his eyes and moans. His nipples feel enormous, throbbing with each heartbeat. The frostbite claws into them, filling them like pincushions with sharp needles of pain. His whole body trembles, but Kip keeps his arms at his sides, clenching fistfuls of air. His cock stands up rigid and shiny red.

Then the ice cube is gone, melted away. Vince's forefinger and thumb choose a nipple to pick on, plucking and pulling at the scalded tip.

"You put out for a lot of guys, don't you?"

The question slides into Kip's consciousness, taking a long muddled detour around the ache in his nipples. "No. Not really—"

"Don't bullshit me, kid. I don't like pussies who lie to me. I saw the way you got down on your knees for it this morning. Couldn't wait to get your mouth all over it. You've gone down before, plenty of times."

"A few ..."

"Oh yeah?" Vince savagely twirls the nipple between his fingernails, making him yelp. "Sucking off the hotel johns for a little cash on the side. You bend over and let those guys stick it up that tight little hole? Or is that just for Uncle Max?" Vince slaps him smartly across the face.

Kip recoils and cringes. "No—I mean, sometimes. But usually, most of them"—he stammers, trying to defend himself—"usually they just ... want to suck me off."

Vince laughs. "You shitting me, pussyboy? Pay to suck this little weenie?" He runs the chilly surface of his glass against Kip's cock, making him gasp. "Must be a pretty desperate bunch of old toads—paying good money to slobber over your stiff little nub." He raises the glass to his lips and swallows. "You know what I think, Kip? I think you're a cocksucker. And a liar. I think you're nothing but a cheap little slut, working the hotel johns to get a stiff dick up your pussy."

Kip tries to answer, but his lips and tongue are suddenly shapeless. Instead he only groans. Then yelps, as Vince slaps him across the mouth.

And then Kip is alone again, blushing nude and erect in the center of the room. Vince has returned to the dresser to pour himself another drink.

"Get your pussy over here, slutboy. On your hands and knees."

Kip drops to all fours, suddenly dizzy and glad to be on the floor. He crawls across the carpet, face stinging, nipples throbbing, until he reaches the heels of the man's shiny black shoes. He stares at them for a long moment. Vince turns around. Kip raises his head slowly.

Above him, Vince looks down and smirks. A fresh cigarette hangs from the corner of his mouth. His fly is open. His big, nude cock hovers over Kip's upturned face, softly swollen and impossibly thick. The dizziness returns. Kip clutches the carpet and moans.

Vince takes a long drag on his cigarette and laughs. "See something you like, pussyboy?"

Kip moans louder, and licks his lips. He stares mesmerized at the massive tube of smooth, naked flesh, displayed luridly before his face. So beautiful. So brutally big. Heavy and blunt, corrugated with veins beneath the sleek, taut wrapping of flesh. Pulsing and growing thicker before his astonished eyes. Suddenly he seems to see the scene from somewhere else in the room: the nude blond boy in a bow tie on his hands and knees; the big man in the business suit above him, lewdly exposing his oversized sex. The man smoking a cigarette casually, taking his time—the boy itchy and hot between his legs, hungry to have it in his mouth. Kip puts on a show for the voyeur in his mind: wiggling his ass, breathing hard, biting his lips. Naked pussyboy, craving cock.

Vince finishes his cigarette and snuffs it out. He leans his ass against the dresser and spreads his feet apart, framing Kip between his legs. The plump, waxy-looking head of his cock hovers inches from the boy's parted lips. Kip feels the heat that radiates from the cockflesh. He watches Vince's heartbeat in the long thick vein that pulses lazily down one side. His nostrils are filled with the odor of the man's sex. He can almost taste it on his tongue.

But instead of cock, Vince feeds him liquor. He uncaps the bottle of bourbon and lowers it to Kip's mouth, pushing his head back and telling him to swallow. He slides the neck of the bottle into the boy's mouth and pours the booze down his throat in long, burning draughts, tilting the bottle up and lowering it, listening to Kip gurgle and cough. Trickles of amber bubble from the corners of Kip's mouth and run in rivulets down his undulating throat, into the hollows of his collarbone and over his shiny, pumped-up pecs, stinging his swollen nipples. Kip's glazed eyes are riveted on the naked shaft, watching it thicken and slowly grow erect alongside the bottle, wishing it were the big cock that Vince was emptying over and over again into his throat.

The bottle is empty. Vince sets it aside and pulls the boy to his feet. Kip moans, wanting to stay close to the big cock. Then hands are gliding over his naked flesh, pulling him close, crushing him against the man's big chest. The hands glide down the small of his back and onto his ass, pulling his buttocks apart—then a finger penetrates his hole and slides knuckle-deep into his rectum. He gasps and looks up into Vince Zorio's smoldering eyes.

Kip

"Ummm. Now I think I'm ready to have some fun with you, pussyboy."

Half past nine: Kip kneels on the hard tile floor of the bathroom in Vince Zorio's suite. His trembling body glistens with a sheen of cold sweat. His legs are folded beneath him. His ass rests on his heels. He is naked, except for the bow tie wrapped snugly around his neck, and the black silk tie that binds his hands behind his back. His throat is filled with Vince's cock. His ass is filled with the enema Vince gave him earlier and the cruelly thick buttplug that holds it inside.

Vince sits on the toilet. He has removed his shirt and jacket. Tufts of wiry black hair sprout above the neckline of his undershirt. His pants and boxer shorts are pushed down to his ankles. His bare feet are planted on either side of the toilet, propping his knees wide apart. His dick is buried deep in Kip's throat.

Kip's jaws ache from sucking cock. His shoulders and arms are stiff and sore from being pulled so tightly behind his back. He cannot seem to stop shaking. The enema rumbles in his guts, making his bowels spasm and knot into wicked cramps. His hard-on would have vanished long ago, except for the thin leather cord tied cutting-tight around his cock. Kip is miserable, on the verge of crying.

He pulls his face from Vince's crotch, letting the cock slide free from his throat. It snaps upward from his lips, ramrod stiff and glossy with saliva. It seems to Kip that he has been sucking on Vince's cock for hours. The big dick never goes soft, never shoots. It towers before him like a harsh rebuke, unsatisfied and demanding to be sucked again.

His bowels are knotted with cramps. He shivers uncontrollably. Beads of sweat erupt across his forehead and trickle down his nose. He stares up at Vince's face, looking for relief, but the big man only smirks.

"Please," Kip begs hoarsely. "Please—take it out of me. Out of my ass. Oh, please. I can't hold it anymore."

Vince smiles. And shakes his head. "You know the rules, pussyboy. You blow me till I come. You suck the cream out of my big, fat dick, and then I pull the plug." Vince grabs the base of his dick and waves it like a billy club, cock-proud and horny. He tilts it down, pointing at Kip's mouth, and rubs the head over the boy's pouting lips. "Well, pussyboy?"

Vince is playing a cruel game with him. Kip knows he has sucked the man to the verge of coming several times already—he can tell from the quickening of Vince's breath, the way his body draws taut, the way his cock expands abruptly and throbs in his throat. But every time Vince shoves his mouth away at the last minute and sits gasping on the toilet, letting the orgasm recede, waiting until his twitching dick has cooled before beginning the game all over again.

Kip sobs. Tears well in his eyes. He has promised himself he will not cry, but he can no longer help it. He opens his mouth, whimpering, and leans forward to suck.

Just as his lips make contact, Vince pulls the cock up and out of reach. He looks at Kip thoughtfully. "Uh-uh. I think I want you to suck on my nuts for a while."

Kip groans. Vince pinches his mouth open and stuffs the big balls inside. He sits back on the toilet and spreads his legs wide open. Kip's cheeks are outrageously bloated. The plump, heavy scrotum fills his mouth. The testicles are alive, twitching and jerking inside the sack. Vince laughs. "You look like a little

Kip

chipmunk, pussyboy. Don't just hold 'em. Use your tongue." Vince strokes his cock slowly and gives himself over to the exquisite sensation....

Kip's mind is so jumbled that he can hardly recall a time when he has not been in bondage on his knees, sucking cock and enduring the enema. Vaguely he remembers how it began—in the other room, long ago, when Vince removed his tie and told Kip to cross his wrists behind his back. Kip was slow to respond, partly from the booze, partly out of fear, but as Vince wrapped the silk cord tight around his wrists, placing him in bondage for the first time in his life, he flushed with an excitement that made him shake. To be standing naked and erect and helpless in the man's room, while Vince slowly circled him, pulling on the big, nude cock that jutted from his open fly and appraising Kip like a newly purchased toy—as if a deeply buried fantasy had somehow erupted into the real world and taken on a dangerous life of its own. Kip was excited. Kip was frightened. Kip was a nude, helpless pussyboy with his hands tied behind his back and his cock standing up stiff between his legs, and Vince Zorio was going to fuck him.

Then the man began to humiliate him, gradually escalating the abuse. Vince liked to use his big, meaty hands. Pinching Kip's swollen nipples. Slapping his face. Punching his belly. Squeezing his ass, hard enough to leave bruises. Stinging his sturdy little erection with hard open-handed slaps.

Vince seemed especially to enjoy abusing his cock. Tying it at the base so that it stood up shiny and red. Swatting it with his hand. Raking his fingernails up the length and pinching the tip. Humiliating it—telling Kip he had a little weenie between his legs. Cradling the weenie in his hand and spanking it with his own huge truncheon of meat, driving home the difference between them. *Humiliate a boy's hard cock,* Vince had once told Battaglia, *and just watch the way his hole opens up for anything you wanna put inside.*

When it came time to clean the boy out, Vince opened the dresser's middle drawer and pulled out an aluminum briefcase. Kip caught a glimpse of the contents and raised his eyebrows in alarm. A yellow enema bag and a coil of tubing. A huge black rubber buttplug. A confusion of items he couldn't name, made of leather, rubber, chrome. And at the back of the briefcase, buried in the tangle but catching the light with the unmistakable glint of cold black steel, a gun ...

A quarter past ten: Vince has decided to come. It seems a shame. Kip is doing such a fine job on his cock. Hard, relentless, deep-throat cocksucking. Nonstop. No sissy-kissing or tongue-lapping. No idling while the boy stops to catch his breath—getting Vince off is infinitely more important than that.

The dark-headed hustler back in Kansas City sucked with the same enthusiasm. So did the blonde bitch in Dallas. So have all the other cocksuckers in all the other towns who have found themselves naked on their knees in a hotel john with Vince Zorio, with an enema up their butts and their hands tied behind their backs. Guaranteed incentive to make certain Vince's cock gets the loving, undivided attention it deserves. A sure ticket to the best blowjob in town—and Vince always treats himself to the best. A UCLA gymnast he picked up at a bar in West Hollywood holds the record—a little over nine-

Kip

ty minutes of desperately fucking his face on Vince's big cock before Vince gave him the load he was begging for and pulled the plug from his ass. Of course, the gymnast had the added incentive of the alligator clamps Vince had attached to his nipples and the tip of his penis.

Vince is up for breaking the record. Kip has worked him up stiff as a girder, and Vince could stay that way all night; he is in no hurry to shoot. But little Kip, for all his natural talent, obviously doesn't have that kind of stamina. The boy is covered with sweat, shaking like a leaf. Whimpering and gagging himself nonstop, his head bouncing up and down like a piston about to blow.

At one point the boy even pissed himself—let go with an uncontrollable spray that jetted straight out of his hard, bound cock and spattered against the front of the toilet. Kip flushed cherry red, but never stopped sucking. Vince has seen it happen before.

Remembering excites him. Vince grabs the base of his dick and whips it out of the kid's mouth.

Kip sobs and groans, thinking Vince is teasing him again. "No," he croaks. "Let me. Put it back—"

"Let you what?"

"Let me suck it." Kip is whining now. Begging. Babbling. "Please—come in my mouth. Oh *please,* put it back—in my mouth—let me suck." The kid is raving, delirious. "I can't—I can't—Please. Fuck me. *Fuck me!"* And he opens his mouth almost frighteningly wide, scrunching his features up against his forehead, making his whole face into a gaping, hungry hole.

Vince is impressed. And almost tempted to prolong the torment. Kip looks so desirable that way. Down on his knees, cringing nude in a pool of his own sweat and urine. Big tits heaving out, tight rump sticking up behind. Blond hair plastered against his forehead. Tears running down his cheeks. Every muscle taut and glazed with sweat. Turning his mouth into a pussy that begs for Vince's dick.

The least Vince can do is shove his cock into that hole and come. Instead, he leans back on the toilet and aims his dick at Kip's wide-open mouth. He breathes deep. Two quick strokes and he's there.

It's a hefty load—after so much sucking, Vince's balls hang heavy as a pair of lemons. He thrashes on the toilet seat, shuddering from the force of the climax. His cock is like a hose, spraying semen all over Kip's gaping face and chest.

He takes his time catching his breath, then slowly gets off the toilet, pulls up his pants, tucks in his undershirt. He leaves his fly open. His emptied balls contract to their normal size, but his cock thrusts out the opening as stiff and ready as if he had never come. Finally he pulls Kip to his feet and grabs the base of the buttplug. He has to screw and tug—it's a tight fit. Then he steps aside, laughing, while Kip scurries crablike onto the commode....

Midnight: Kip lies on the bed. The sheets are wildly rumpled, soaked with sweat. He is hog-tied, wrist to ankle—arms pulled down alongside his body, legs folded beneath him, knees apart. He began that way at the foot of the bed, with his ass hanging over the edge, an easy target for Vince's dick. Now he is jammed sideways against the headboard, neck bent, face pressed against the wood. Over the past two hours, Vince has ridden him up and down and across the bed a dozen times.

Vince stands at the side of the bed, facing Kip's ass, naked except for his undershirt. The thin, ribbed cotton is almost transparent with sweat, clinging to his broad chest and back. His satisfied, rubbery cock droops heavily from his crotch, coated with shiny mucus and oozing semen from the tip. In his hand he holds a wire coat hanger, untwisted at the top and crudely straightened like a long, thin shepherd's crook.

The wire hanger has done a good job. Vince was lucky to find it. The hotel hangers are all made of wood, but high on a shelf in the closet, left over from a previous guest's dry cleaning, he came across the tool he was looking for.

He would have preferred using his belt. But belts are noisy.

So are boys in the process of having their asses whipped. Which is why the buttplug that earlier held his enema inside is now stuffed into Kip's wide-open mouth, held in place by a bandanna made from his own nylon panties. Kip's face is red from the strain and wet from crying.

Kip's ass is pushed outward and up, taut as a drumhead. So wide open that the deep cleft between his cheeks is flattened and his hole rudely exposed, completely vulnerable. The pale, silky bottom flesh sizzles with thin red welts. The bud of his anus is equally red and chafed, distended and swollen like a bee sting, the tender lips rubbed raw by long, relentless fucking.

Vince reaches for the phone on the bedside table and dials the switchboard. While he waits, he prods Kip's ass with the blunt, hooked end of the coat hanger. Kip's grunt is muffled by the buttplug. Vince snakes the hanger between the boy's thighs and hooks his cock, pulling it backward between his legs. Still hard as a rock.

"Yeah, operator. Suite 1505. I want you to ring the phone in the adjoining bedroom."

Vince pulls the hanger upward and back, seeing how far the stubby shaft will bend. Another inch and it snaps free, slapping up against the kid's belly. Kip moans.

"Leo—I saw the light go on under your door a while back. Getting in kinda late, aren't you? Yeah. So how were the chicks down on pussy boulevard? No such luck, huh? You're a crazy sonofabitch to be out on the streets tonight anyway, not with all the heat. Yeah, tell me about it—always horny as hell after a job. Especially like the bitch we pulled today."

Kip turns his head, realizing only gradually that Vince is speaking to someone else.

"Nah, stayed in all night. Found my piece on the premises. Yeah, you know me. Sure, come on over."

Kip stiffens, suddenly understanding.

Vince is in the bathroom, pissing, when the door to the adjoining bedroom swings open. Pressed against the headboard, Kip can see nothing. But he feels the stranger's presence in the room, somewhere behind him, drawing closer; then hears the toilet flush, and Vince returning.

"Jesus, Vince, you sure did a job on his ass." The voice is deep and detached, faintly sarcastic; delivered from the corner of the mouth, with a more pronounced New York accent than Vince's.

"Yeah." The sound of a striking match—Vince lighting a cigarette.

"And such a pretty ass it is. So what does the rest of him look like?"

Vince seizes Kip by the hair and twists him around.

Above him stands a giant of a man. Thick featured, rumple faced, with a broad, flattened nose. Heavyset and balding. He wears a long purple satin robe and smokes a cigar. A gold necklace hangs from his bull-like neck, almost buried in bristling black hair. Rings glitter on both hands.

Leo Battaglia looks down at the bound boy with the buttplug in his mouth and the bow tie around his throat. He sneers and shakes his head. "Ah, Vincent, you're gonna burn in hell for this kind of shit. You and your boys. But I gotta admit—you know how to pick 'em. Pretty as a girl. And such big titties. You always go for the blonds with big tits, no matter what they got between their legs."

Vince shrugs, smiling faintly. "What they all got between their legs, Leo, is a nice, sweet hole."

Leo snorts. "So where'd you find the little cocksucker—in the hotel, you said?"

"Room-service waiter. Delivered a blowjob with breakfast. Came back for more. Just a hustler, really. Works the hotel johns."

Leo cups the boy's chin. Kip meets his stare for an instant, and shudders. Leo runs his thumb in a circle around the rim of the buttplug, grazing the boy's puffy, swollen lips.

"Good mouth?"

Vince kisses his fingertips. *"Perfetto.* Try it on for size."

"You sure we oughta pull out the gag? What if he starts yelling?"

"No sweat. He's plenty softened up by now. Besides, he's got a sugar daddy on the staff. Uncle Max might just about shit his pants if he could see you now—right, Kip?"

Leo nods. He unties the sash at his waist and lets the robe fall.

The utter corpulence of the man's nudity overwhelms Kip. At one time, Leo Battaglia possessed a magnificent physique; in his youth he must have been godlike. But there is nothing beautiful about his body now. Leo is an awesome wreckage of a man, still muscular but long gone to seed. Enormous slablike shoulders, powerful arms. Big, fleshy tits and a hard, overhanging belly. Swirls of kinky black hair carpet his stomach and chest. His body exudes a crude, intoxicating aura of overpowering maleness; virile, overripe sensuality oozes from every pore. Beside him, Kip feels small and ridiculous, trussed up naked and dribbling saliva around the plug in his mouth.

Kip looks down, between Leo's legs. His eyes widen in alarm. He had hoped Leo might have a small cock, at least smaller than Vince's, easy to accommodate and satisfy. But Kip is out of luck. And the night is just beginning....

Five o'clock in the morning: Kip lies on the bed, on his side. His mind and body are exhausted. He can hardly move. But he is no longer bound. He might leave now, escape from the room. But Kip is going nowhere. Because Vince is inside him. The man lies behind him on the bed, pressed against Kip's back, joined by a glue of sweat and semen. His cock is lodged deep in the boy's ass, holding him impaled like a fish on a hook. He nuzzles the back of Kip's neck, grazing it with his lips, nipping gently with his teeth.

They are alone, and the room is dark and quiet, except for the low mewling sounds that Kip occasionally makes, like a puppy whimpering in its sleep. Leo has come and gone. Come twice: once in Kip's ass, once in his mouth.

Kip's mind is neither awake nor asleep, but motionless, running in place. The eternity of the past few hours replays itself over and over in his head. Leo's huge, gnarled cock in his mouth. The wire hanger slashing out of nowhere against his already-

Kip

punished ass—the memory makes him flinch—and the vibrations of Kip's muffled scream coursing through the man's dick, making it tingle. Leo liked the effect. Vince obliged, wielding the hanger with his strong right arm. They traded places. Leo whipped even harder than Vince.

Then they moved on to another game.

Leo seldom fucked ass. At least not boyass. That's what he said. But Kip was the exception. Vince and Leo double-dicked him like seasoned partners, one of them screwing his mouth, the other his rear, pulling out to trade places again and again, until Kip hardly knew which man fucked him and which man he sucked. His body was a long continuous tube, plugged with thick cock at both ends. Eventually they untied him. Leo said something about getting his gun to make sure the kid didn't bolt. The words hardly registered on Kip's exhausted brain, but Vince snapped at Leo to shut up. "You're gonna really fuck us up one of these days, Battaglia. You're always too fucking careless with your mouth...."

But his anger cooled quickly as they returned to using Kip. To satisfy Leo, he retied Kip's hands behind his back. They put him on his knees, then took their places at opposite ends of the room and made him crawl stupefied from cock to cock. When one of them had finished with him for the moment, he would shove the boy away, and Kip would shuffle awkwardly to the other, scraping his knees against the carpet until they were raw. Depending on the hole preferred, he would bow his head to suck, or else turn around and stagger to his feet, squatting back to take the waiting cock up his ass while the man across the room watched and pulled on his own freshly serviced dick.

When Kip suddenly came to a standstill in the

middle of the room, unable to go on and begging them to let him rest, Vince reached for the hanger. Kip continued to crawl, miles and miles without ever leaving the room.

At some point, hazy in Kip's memory, Leo finally left, returning to his own room, leaving the taste of his oily semen warm and fresh on Kip's tongue.

Then the evening wound down and contracted to a single spot, concentrated at the point where Vince's cock is now snugly lodged inside the boy's well-worked hole....

The cock is deeply rooted—almost motionless—but Kip's ass is so tender that the least movement sends twinges of sensation through his crammed bowels. He can feel each beat of Vince's heart from the veins that throb against his rectal walls.

Vince plays his passive body like an instrument, making him whimper and squirm. His caresses are slow, calculated, tender—but Kip's raw flesh is so acutely tuned that even the most delicate touch courses through him like the crack of a whip. Vince runs his fingertips over Kip's nipples, down the ridges of his belly. The boy quivers in response. He squeezes the swollen head of Kip's cock gently, and strokes the shaft once with his forefinger and thumb. Kip shudders, on the verge of coming. Vince flicks his finger against the boy's balls, seizes a hair, and slowly, slowly plucks it—Kip's rectum convulses around the man's cock. Vince runs his hand over the boy's hip, onto his ass, and plays his fingertips across the welts, like a blind man reading braille. His other hand, circling Kip from below, finds a nipple to twist gently. Kip writhes in the man's embrace and squeezes his ass around the big, inexhaustible cock with a slow, steady rhythm.

For Vince, this is the best of all fucks. The final

screw. A tenderized hole that throbs around his dick. A boy who quivers like a bowstring in his arms at the least whisper of a touch. It has taken all night to bring Kip to this point. The effort is always worth it.

A pale blue light shows through the heavy drapes. Dawn, and soon Vince will have to end it. Kip is the best he's had in months. He could easily spend a week working the kid over, or a month, grinding him harder and harder beneath his heel, seeing just how deep the boy's hunger dwells. But Vince has an early morning flight to catch; and now that the job is done, there is no reason to stay and every reason to leave.

Soon he will come in the boy's ass, for the final time. And then, to milk the last few drops from his cock, he will finally bring Kip off. The boy's cock is primed to bursting, and has been for hours. A single stroke will do it—a glide of his fingernail down the underbelly of Kip's cock, and the stubby little erection will give a twitch and suddenly explode.

And then—

Vince hears a noise.

In the hallway. Muffled steps. Someone walking up the hall. Not *someone*—the noise is too complicated to come from a lone walker, or even two. A group of people coming up the hall. Vince goes rigid, wide awake.

A sound at the door. Not the normal jangling of a key in a lock, but quiet, methodical—a stalking, covert sound.

He is off the bed in an instant. He takes Kip with him, keeping his cock in the boy's ass as he bolts toward the dresser and fumbles in the open briefcase for his gun. Kip squeals in protest—the swirling movement dizzies him, the sudden jogging of the cock in his ass threatens to send him over the edge. The gun flashes in the corner of his eye and he stiffens in fear, groggy and confused, but coming rapidly to his senses.

The door to the room bursts open, ripping the chain lock from the wall. Almost instantly the overhead light flashes on, blinding after the darkness, as they rush into the room—a man in plainclothes and behind him uniformed police, at least five of them, more in the hallway, all holding guns.

There is a frozen moment of shock on all sides.

Vince's arm is locked across Kip's chest. His cock is still in the boy's ass, throbbing with a jackrabbit pulse. He holds the gun to Kip's throat.

"My, my." The plainclothesman finally speaks. The room seethes with tension, but the man sounds bored, covering his agitation with studied finesse. He shakes his head. "We knew you was a killer, Zorio. But I had no idea …"

Kip's whole body prickles with heat. He cannot escape. There is no way to hide. He feels the eyes of all the men rake over his naked body, hoisted to tiptoes on Vince's cock. He hears them murmur in shock and derision. Pussyboy, caught in the act. His cock juts stiffly from his hips for all to see, quivering and closer than ever to coming.

The plainclothesman speaks slowly, deliberately, getting down to business. "Come on, Zorio. There's no way out of this hole. We got half the department down in the lobby. And the rest are taking a coffee break across the street. Come on. You don't wanna hurt the kid."

Vince stands stock-still, breathing hard. His heartbeat pounds like a fist against Kip's back. And then it happens. Kip cannot stop it. He tries desperately to cover himself with his hands, but his arms are pinned to his sides. His cock twitches and bobs in the air, and then begins to shoot—long, spiraling ribbons of stored-up semen that jet halfway across the room, landing with a dull splat on the carpet before the plainclothesman's feet. He writhes helplessly in Vince's hold, jerking weirdly like a puppet. The ordeal seems to go on forever. The officers stare speechless. One of them mutters, "Holy shit!"

Behind Vince, the door to Battaglia's room bursts open. Vince whirls half-way round. A confusion of sudden movement and shouting—*"Watch out!"*—then the deafening blast of pistol fire, three times in rapid succession.

With each shot, Vince convulses in a horrible parody of fucking Kip's ass. He staggers forward, his weight bowing Kip's shoulders, then falls back. His softening cock pulls out of Kip's bowels with a loud, liquid fart. His body slams the floor with a thud that reverberates into the soles of Kip's feet.

Kip swings around, his cock still twitching and dribbling. For an instant he sees the motionless hulk of Vince's body, lying flat on his back with a strange surly grimace on his face, his eyes wide open. Then the cops are everywhere, a swirling sea of blue, and the plainclothesman is on him, grabbing Kip by the shoulders and steering him toward the door to Battaglia's room. "No," Kip whispers dully, looking over his shoulder, "no …"

There are more cops in the other room, and Leo, standing handcuffed in his purple robe, his big ugly face made even uglier by the unexpected tears gushing over his rumpled jowls. The cops, flushed with triumph, are startled at the sight of Kip, then rally with whistles and jeers. "Can it," the plainclothesman says. He yanks the spread from Leo's bed and wraps it over Kip's shoulders.

With the bedspread folded around him, Kip stands mute and numb as a refugee, shivering uncontrollably. The plainclothesman speaks softly, asking him something, but Kip does not hear. He turns and stares into the other room. Through the narrow frame of the doorway, he can see only Vince's legs and feet. Then a blanket descends, and only the feet are visible. And then, as the policemen swarm, even the feet are lost to sight, obscured by a maze of blue trousers and shiny black boots.

» THE VICE «

From the police physician's report: *"Patient a 19-year-old Caucasian youth. Blond, blue-eyed, 5'9", approximately 150 pounds. Victim of rape. Trauma in both throat and rectum indicate rough and repeated intrusions. Large quantities of semen in rectum. Some difficulty in walking; probably due to stiffness in legs, as well as trauma to rectum. Visible injuries include swelling and contusions around lips, nipples, and anus. Numerous bruises in pelvic region—appear to have been made by hands gripping his hips from behind. Numerous markings across buttocks; patient indicates they were caused by a wire coat hanger. Marks are concentrated around the immediate exterior of the patient's anus with some across the anus itself. Chafing around the patient's wrists and lingering numbness in his digits, caused by a man's tie used to bind his wrists; this also accounts for muscular ache in his shoulders and back. Patient also complains of abdominal cramps and is noticeably flatulent. Assume due to prolonged and repeated trauma to rectum (loss of sphincter control), as well as to a large enema (tapwater) administered prior to his initial rape; victim was made to hold enema 'for a real long time.' Patient will recover...."*

Kip wakes with a shiver and a start. The bedroom is flooded with light. He glances at the bedside clock: twelve noon. He must have switched off the alarm without waking. That happens a lot these days.

It was the dream that finally woke him. The same nightmare that wakes him almost every morning, or sometimes in the middle of the night. The dream in which he's trapped again in the hotel room with Vince Zorio.

Nude. Helpless. Trembling and weak from the long night of brutal sex, his mouth and asshole raped over and over by Zorio's huge, unrelenting cock, while Zorio slaps his balls and stings his nipples and whispers around the tongue that slithers in Kip's ear, just another hole to be fucked, calling him Pussyboy, Slutboy, Cocksucker ...

The sudden crash at the door. The sea of blue that floods the room. Hoisted clear off the bed on Zorio's giant cock and lifted to his feet, paraded on tiptoe before the line of blue-clad policemen who suddenly jam the room, leering at the spectacle with mouths agape—all of them staring and sniggering while Vince holds the gun to Kip's head and continues to fuck him, making him jerk and twitch like a boy-marionette impaled on a stick.

And then the most shameful moment of his life, as Kip begins to come, out of control, unable to stop it, ribbons of semen squirting from his untouched cock, landing with a splat at the plainclothesman's feet. The policemen purse their lips and shake their heads in amazement and disgust.....

And then—terrible, total confusion. Gunshots. Panic. And even as the semen keeps spurting from Kip's cock, Zorio slides out of him, the huge cock oozing from his burning ass like a long, hard turd, exiting with a liquid plop. Zorio collapses heavily to the floor, as crumpled and lifeless as any other corpse....

Kip shuts his eyes tight, but opens them quickly, afraid the nightmare will return. Mouth dry. Heart pounding in his chest. Breathing rapid and shallow. The sheets around him are soaked with sweat, clinging to his naked skin. He peels them away, throws back the cover, looks down at his body. At his heaving chest, finely etched with muscle, slick with sweat, porcelain-smooth except for the oversized nipples drawn up pointed and erect. At the hard muscles clustered around his navel, knotted with tension. At his cock, jabbing upward from his groin and curving back to point toward his navel, so hard it quivers like a plucked bowstring in the air.

He rolls over, dragging the sheets with him, tangling his legs, settling on his chest and belly and humping the moist sheets, sliding his cock in a groove against the mattress. Always the same. He wakes from the nightmare with his heart racing, his body drenched with cold sweat—and his cock so hard it hurts.

It's been three months since that night—the night Kip spent in Vince Zorio's hotel room, the night that ended with Kip's public humiliation and Zorio's death.

Was it rape? It was the police who first suggested the word. Perhaps they just couldn't imagine that any young man would have submitted willingly to the cruelties that Zorio inflicted on Kip that night. Or perhaps they were just trying to give Kip an easy way out, a way to pretend it all happened against his will. But his hands had been free when the police arrived. And his cock had been hard—so hard that he came without touching himself, just from the fact of having Vince Zorio inside him while a roomful of men looked on and gaped. As hard as it is at this moment, lying naked in his bed and reliving the incident for the thousandth time.

Three months—and Kip is still shaky, still far from being over it. Fortunately, Uncle Max has been very understanding. Of course, if Max could have seen Kip in the middle of having sex with Zorio—crawling on his hands and knees, begging to suck the big man's cock—his compassion might fade in an instant, twisted into jealousy. But Max seems almost eager to accept the official version of the incident, the one that has Kip playing the utter innocent, an unsuspecting room-service waiter lured into a hit man's room, physically subdued and then repeatedly, brutally, raped against his will.

And Leo. Kip has never mentioned the part Leo played, not even to the cops. The cops have never asked, and Kip would be too ashamed to volunteer it. Leo Battaglia. Giant Leo—gray, corpulent, massively hung. The man Vince called his partner, staying in the suite's adjoining bedroom. Somewhere in the middle of that night, Leo had entered the picture, joined in the fun. The two of them had worked Kip over like seasoned pros, running him ragged, sending him crawling from cock to cock, double-dicking him from both ends—stuffing both holes at once and then changing places. Leo had been every bit as cruel as Vince, every bit as demanding. But he lacked Vince's stamina. Leo had come and gone—come twice, first in Kip's ass, and then in his mouth. Then disappeared back into his half of the suite, not to reappear until the last scene, the final showdown ...

And, of course, Kip has made no mention of how and when it all begin. Before that night there had been the morning, when Kip delivered Zorio's breakfast—and a blowjob to go along with it. Or the fact that Zorio had paid Kip for sucking him off and promised more money for coming back that night. Or that other hotel guests had paid him in the past for the chance to put their cocks down his throat or up his ass. Of course, Kip would have done it with or without the money....

Slutboy. That's what Zorio had called him. *Sucking off the hotel johns for a little cash on the side. You bend over and let those guys stick it up that tight little hole? Nothing but a cheap little slut, working the johns to get a stiff dick up your pussy ...*

And all the while, sweet Uncle Max thought he was the only one with a key to Kip's box. There Max would be, whistling while he worked down in the hotel kitchen, smiling at the staff and making them wonder what put him in such a good mood as he thought of his nephew's sweet, tight butt and hungry mouth, treasures no one else had ever known, moist, slick holes made to please his cock alone—and meanwhile Kip would be squealing and grunting in a dim bedroom somewhere high above, bent over a dresser with his pants around his ankles and his face pressed to the mirror while some fat traveling salesman, puffing and sweating, screwed Kip's ass and blubbered in his ear and ran his fingers through the boy's silky blond hair ...

No, it was better that Uncle Max never know what Kip had been up to, long before Vince Zorio entered the picture. And better that he never guess how badly Kip had craved it that night from Leo and Vince.

Since the incident, Max has left Kip completely alone, dropping only the vaguest hints that he should return to work sometime—but no bother, Max wouldn't think of rushing the boy; he understands that Kip needs time to work things out.

Max has left him alone in bed as well. Hasn't laid a finger on him since the incident. No more tiptoeing across the apartment into Kip's little room in the middle of the night, pulling back the sheets in utter darkness, running his sweaty palms up the boy's sleek thighs until he finds a hole to slide his finger in—grabbing the sleepy, squirming boy by the hips and flipping him over onto his belly, using his middle finger like a pivot up Kip's ass—then pulling it out with a pop and hurriedly replacing it with his cock, mounting him without a word while Kip buries his face in the pillows and moans and pushes back for more. No more waking Kip up in the morning by gently batting his cock against the boy's soft pink lips until he blinks and yawns and finds himself with a mouthful of Uncle Max's meat. Since the incident Max has drawn away, holding himself back with an almost visible restraint. Perhaps he feels guilty somehow.

Sometimes Kip wishes Max would get over his new shyness and use him again. It was never as exciting with Max as with the other men, the hotel guests, the anonymous strangers passing through; nowhere near as thrilling as it had been with Vince or even with Leo Battaglia. But Kip would gladly settle for it. Kip needs the human contact. Kip needs to be fucked, even though he fears it now.

One night the hunger and confusion grew so great he pulled himself from bed, walked across the apart-

Kip

ment and into the master bedroom and found himself standing nude and erect at the foot of the big plush bed, whispering: *Fuck me, Uncle Max. Please. I need it, sir, so bad. I need your cock up my ass. In my throat. Fuck me, please, Uncle Max.* Kip's nipples drew up tingling and erect. His ass grew loose and itchy. His cock stood up hard as rubber. He could hardly speak for the sudden thickness in his throat, and the trembling. *Punish me, Uncle Max. I've been a bad boy. A pussyboy. A boy with a wide-open hole for any man who wants to fuck it. Punish me, please, Uncle Max. Please, sir—fuck my pussy....*

But Max had never awakened, had just kept loudly snoring. Finally, his face burning with shame, Kip ran back to his own bed and masturbated for hours, sticking fingers up his hole, coming over and over until dawn, all the while imagining Vince Zorio standing beside the bed. Vince—stripped to the waist, a cigarette dangling from his smirking lips, a look of utter contempt in his cool gray eyes. A long leather belt dangling from his fist, his muscular chest rising and falling from the exertion of swinging it. That huge truncheon of flesh dangling from his open fly, beer-bottle thick, bloated and shiny from fucking a pussyboy who just keeps begging for more ...

There is a very loud knock at the apartment's front door.

In an instant, Kip realizes that it wasn't the dream that woke him this time, but the knocking. Not the deafening blast of the bullets ripping into Zorio's back in his nightmare, but the loud, insistent banging.

He rolls over and pulls the pillows around his ears. His hard-on throbs between his legs. The banging stops. Silence. Kip sighs and slides his hand over his chest and belly, down towards his aching erection.

Whoever it was will just have to come back some other time.

But the knocking resumes. So loud that it sounds almost as if it comes from his own bedroom door. Knocking as if the building were on fire.

Kip drags himself from the warm bed and searches for his housecoat. He bumps his knee against the foot of the bed, winces, and reaches down to soothe it, his hard cock slapping up and down against his belly. He finds the robe draped over a chair, a red silk kimono imported from Japan—a gift from Uncle Max. He pushes his arms into the loose billowing sleeves, pulls the flaps over his chest.

The robe is cut very short, just a half-coat really, showing off plenty of thigh—the way Uncle Max likes to see him around the house. His hard-on pokes up against the thin silk like a tent pole, then pops through the flaps. Kip catches a glimpse of it in the mirror—like a tiny pink worm emerging from a field of red, pale and quivering. He blushes. He remembers Vince, flaunting his own obscenely huge cock, making fun of Kip for having such a useless little weenie....

The banging continues, rattling his nerves. He should put on some briefs before his answers the door. He stumbles to the dresser, opens a drawer, reaches blindly inside, and pulls out a pair. He bends to step into them and suddenly freezes.

By chance, he reached into the wrong drawer. Not the one where he keeps his underwear and socks, but the drawer beside it, where he keeps more private things: a jar of Vaseline, his collection of muscle magazines, a tattered yellow paperback stolen from Uncle Max's closet titled *Bathhouse Bondage*.

And his panties.

That's what Zorio had called them: *Well, well, you*

Kip

dress up special for the occasion—or do all you bellboys wear panties under your outfits?

Kip flushes, remembering. The briefs are sheer black nylon, obscenely skimpy, lewdly suggestive. *The Cupcake Thong,* the catalogue had called them, *for the young male beauty with his assets in the rear.* In other words: lingerie for boys who take it up the ass. Fuck-me panties for the pussyboy in your life. The same pair that Kip wore that night, the night Vince Zorio made him mince across the room, and then crawl, wearing nothing but his black panties, his uniform bow tie, and an all-over blush. Sometimes Kip takes them out and wears them while he masturbates, remembering how it was with Vince. Standing hot and sweaty in front of his mirror, seeing for himself what made Zorio's huge cock stand up so swollen and stiff ...

He begins to step out of the briefs, thinking to put them back and get another pair. Then the banging starts again, making it impossible to think. Who bangs on a door like that? Kip hears a shout behind the banging, a deep voice too low to make out—something about the police? Kip feels a sudden catch in his throat, a strange *déjà vu.*

He struggles to step out of the black nylon briefs, then gives up and slides them over his hips. The fabric is silky against his thighs, tight and pinching in the crotch, lifting and separating his buttocks as it digs into the crack of his ass. He has to bend his hard-on sideways and cramp his balls to stuff them inside.

He walks into the hallway, pulls the robe around him and belts it. Into the living room, where his bare feet sink into deep plush. Up to the door. The banging is deafening.

Suddenly Kip is afraid. He makes sure the chain is in place. Even so, he hesitates, biting his knuckles.

Perhaps they'll go away ... then the banging starts again. He unbolts the door and opens it until the chain pulls taut, leans forward and peers into the dim hallway.

He can make out only a silhouette. A tall man, dressed in an overcoat and tie, wearing a hat. The brim of the hat casts his face in darkness; only the tip of his nose and his cheekbones, sharp and prominent and starkly lit from above, emerge from the shadow of his face.

"Who—"

"Fagan. Lieutenant Karl Fagan. Police. Vice squad."

A badge is thrust into the breach, right against Kip's nose. He draws back, stares at it. The badge is genuine. Kip has seen enough of them in the last three months to know.

"But what—"

"Just a word with you. If you don't mind. If you're not too busy at the moment." The deep voice is slow and unctuous. Phony. Wheedling. The ever-so-faintly sarcastic voice of a man used to dealing with pimps and pushers and whores. Kip senses it all in an instant. Kip is instantly afraid.

"But who do you—what is it you want?"

The badge disappears. The man tilts his head back. A wedge of light falls over the lower half of his face. His jaw is big and square, his mouth broad, with fleshy, sensuous lips. His cheekbones are high and sharp. A long jagged scar runs diagonally across one cheek. His lips compress into a tight, unfriendly smile.

"Why don't you just let me in, kid? Then I can fill you in on all the details."

Kip hesitates. He reaches toward the chain, then falters.

Kip

"Come on, kid. Unlock the door. *Now.*"

Kip closes the door and unlatches the chain. Afraid to let the man in. Afraid not to. He reaches down to turn the knob, but the man is already pushing his way in, knocking Kip to the side. He slams the door behind him.

"Look, mister—" Kip's voice quavers.

"Call me Fagan, kid. Or sir." The cop gives him a steely glance, then turns away, as if dismissing him. He walks around the living room, peering up and down, running a finger over the mantelpiece as if inspecting it for dust. "So where's your Uncle Max, kid?"

"At work." Kip stares at the man's back, big and broad-shouldered inside his trench coat. He shifts nervously from foot to foot, blinking away the last residue of sleep, trying to pull the flimsy robe more tightly about him.

"Oh, yeah—down at the hotel? Quite a place, from what I hear. Really swank. Your Uncle Max is head chef these days, right? Must make a pretty good living." Fagan picks up a piece of bronze sculpture from the mantle, a tacky miniature of Michelangelo's David. The whole apartment is filled with ugly, expensive bric-a-brac. Flocked wallpaper, phony antiques, mirrors in gilded frames. Max is a queen from the old school.

Fagan holds the David in his hands, fondling it idly. "It was your Uncle Max who got you the job down at the hotel, wasn't it?"

"Yeah." Kip lowers his eyes. "Yes, sir."

"Why aren't you there now? Vacation?"

"No." Kip shrugs. "Just taking some time off."

"Oh yeah? Recuperating?" Fagan's voice oozes with insinuation.

"Just ... some time off, that's all." Kip bites his lip,

confused. All the others—the ones who wanted to know about Zorio—were from homicide or the organized-crime detail. Yet Fagan says he's from vice....

Fagan purses his lips and gazes down at the statuette. He skims his middle finger up the crease of its buttocks lightly, then replaces it carelessly on the mantel. The little David faces the wall like a naughty boy, its lean, shapely ass displayed to the room.

"So just what is it you do down at the hotel, Kip?"

Kip is uneasy, hearing his name from the vice cop's lips. How does Fagan know his name, or where he works? What does he want with Max—or with Kip? Kip swallows and takes a deep breath. He steels himself and manages to look the man straight in the eye. "Look, mister, do you have a warrant or something? Because if you don't, I think maybe you should leave."

"Oh, yeah?" Fagan raises one eyebrow. A thin smile twitches across his lips. "Is that so?" He pushes himself away from the mantel and approaches slowly, step by step, staring Kip up and down. His eyes linger on the boy's naked thighs, then rove upward, studying the sheer panels of silk that cling to Kip's chest, molded to the contours of his wide swimmer's pecs, highlighting the big, soft nipples beneath. Kip steps back, trying again, without success, to pull the kimono more tightly about him.

Fagan backs him against the wall. So close that Kip can hear the man's breath, and feel it on his face. Fagan is a big man, six-foot-three, maybe taller. Kip finds it hard to lift his face that high. Instead he finds himself staring down at Fagan's hands. Big, meaty hands, with broad, flat palms and calloused knuckles. The hands of a pimp, or a vice cop. Hands made for slapping, punching, pounding. Why did Kip ever let him in the door?

Kip

"You think I should go, huh?"

"Yes. Please?" Kip's voice breaks, going high and squeaky. His face turns hot.

Fagan raises his hand. Kip flinches—but the man is simply reaching up to finger his ruby-studded tiepin. "I think you should answer my question, Kip. I think you *better* answer it. Just what is it you do down at that swank hotel?"

"I work for Max. On the kitchen staff. A waiter—room service."

Fagan is silent, expressionless. Waiting for more.

"That's all," Kip finally whispers. "I'm a room-service waiter."

"Oh yeah? And just what kind of services do you deliver?"

"Just—the usual."

"The usual what?"

"Dinner, lunch. Breakfast."

"Like the breakfast you delivered to Vince Zorio? Only it seems like you were the one who did most of the eating. Yeah, the way I hear it, you made a real pig of yourself."

Kip sucks in his breath and turns aside. "I don't know what you're talking about." His voice quavers—then turns to a squeal as Fagan spins him about and grabs his jaw in a viselike grip, steely fingers grinding into cartilage and bone.

"Get this straight *right now*, kid—you never lie to me. You lie to your johns if want, if you think you can squeeze 'em for a little more green that way. You lie to your sweet Uncle Maxwell—tell him how it feels *soooo* good while he's porking your butt. But you never lie to Karl Fagan. *Never.* Not if you want to wake up with a dick and two balls between your legs in the morning." Fagan squeezes hard, sending an agonizing jolt through Kip's jaw. "Understand?"

Kip is paralyzed, pulled up to his toes by the man's grip. Fagan forces him to nod, painfully wrenching the boy's face up and down. "Good," Fagan croons. "Smart boy."

Fagan shoves him backward against the wall. Kip crumples against it, reaching up to soothe his jaw with both hands. He looks up, eyes bright with tears. "Please, mister. Who are you? What do you want?"

"Shut up, kid. I'm not here to talk about me. I'm here to talk about you—and your future. And I told you once already: don't call me mister. I'm not one of your faggot johns off the street, you got that, punk? What did I tell you to call me?"

"Fagan," Kip whispers. "Sir."

Fagan nods. "That's better." He smiles, and reaches out. Kip flinches, shutting his eyes tight as Fagan brushes the back of his hand over the boy's cheek, his big, rough knuckles gliding over smooth, downy flesh moistened by a tear. "You're pretty when you're scared, you know that? Pretty little thing. Pretty as a girl. Keep that up, you're gonna give me a hard-on for sure."

Kip blushes and lowers his face. Fagan laughs, then turns and scans the room. "You got any liquor in this place?"

"Yes. Yes, sir."

"Be a good boy—fix Fagan a drink. Whiskey and soda. I'll bet Uncle Max keeps some good whiskey around."

Kip pushes himself from the wall and walks to the bar, his legs unsteady. He suddenly feels ridiculous in the sheer black panties and skimpy robe. Exposed and vulnerable. Embarrassed. Excited. The way he feels when Max comes home with some new outfit for him to model around the apartment—see-through swim trunks, skintight cycling shorts, scoop-neck tank tops cut so low they leave his big nipples bare. The way he felt that night with Zorio ...

Suddenly Kip's skin is hot and acutely sensitive. The red silk drags against his nipples, irritating them, making them crinkle and swell. The tiny briefs cramp his genitals, pinch the tender flesh beneath his balls, ride up the crack of his ass and tickle his hole.

His hands shake as he fixes the drink—ice cubes tinkle against the glass, loud in the plush-carpet silence of the room. When he turns back, Fagan has removed his hat and overcoat.

The man leans casually against one arm of the red velvet sofa in the center of the living room. A big man—he makes the room seem small. Makes Max's gaudy clutter of bric-a-brac look tacky indeed, busy and cheap compared to the absolute simplicity of his face, all sharp angles, tendons, bones. Fagan's eyes glitter like flint, very dark and set deep beneath wide, brooding brows. His hair is fine and dirty blond, parted on the side and greased. In full light, the scar across his cheek is quite prominent. Looking at him, Kip is baffled, uncertain whether Fagan is young or old, handsome or ugly. He only knows that when he looks at Fagan, something quails inside him, frightened to the bone.

He walks across the room, eyes averted, and offers the drink. Fagan stares at the glass.

"Did I tell you to put ice in it?"

Kip's heartbeat accelerates. He feels the pulse in his throat. He feels it in his cock. "No. No, sir."

A long pause—then Fagan takes the drink. Kip bites his lip and breathes in a sigh of relief. But the sigh catches in his throat as Fagan rotates the glass slowly and dumps it, ice and all, onto the cream-colored carpet.

"You can clean up the mess later," Fagan says.

"Now get me what I asked for."

He shoves the glass back at Kip. Kip takes it in both hands, staring dumbly at the empty glass and the widening circle of darkness on the carpet below. Max will be furious; the stain will never come out. He backs away, turns his head sidelong. "Look ... please ... I don't know what you want—"

"Sure you do, kid. You know what I want." Fagan looks him up and down, a smile at the corner of his mouth, his eyes dull and burning. The look is like a touch, clammy and chill. Kip shivers. "You know what I want because I just told you. Twice. A whiskey and soda." Fagan stands, looming over him. "Now fetch it for me, Kip. Before you make me mad."

Kip pauses, biting his lip, trying to still the trembling in his legs. He tries to look up at Fagan's face. Tries to say something. Then gives up. He slowly walks to the bar, mixes the drink, returns. Fagan takes it and tilts it up, finishing half in a single draught. He swirls the glass loosely in his hand and begins to pace.

"I'm here, Kip, because we got word down at vice about your activities at the hotel."

Kip furrows his brow. "I don't know what—"

"Shut your mouth, kid. You're in enough trouble already. Like I said, we heard about your operation downtown. You and your pimp, your precious Uncle Max." Fagan shakes his head in disgust. "What kind of man makes a prostitute out of his own nephew?" He pauses, his eyes roaming up the sturdy, supple curvature of Kip's bottom. "Of course, what kind of man would fuck his own sister's son in the ass?"

Kip feels a chill up his spine. "No, you got it all wrong."

"Oh, yeah? You're telling me you've never bent

over for Uncle Max? Never let him screw his dick up that sweet little hole between your legs?"

Kip blushes. Fagan nods. "That's what I thought."

"No, but he's not—he doesn't know anything about—"

"About what, Kip? About you whoring for the hotel johns? Tell me another one. He sets you up, right? Sends you up to deliver dinner—and a little pussy on the side. You two got a pretty smart thing going. He set you up with Vince Zorio, didn't he? Only he didn't know what kind of shit he was getting you into. Or didn't care."

"No, it's not like that at all. Uncle Max didn't know anything about Zorio. Neither did I." Kip closes his eyes, seeing the lie form in his head like a movie on a screen. "He made me do it."

Fagan laughs out loud. "Who, Zorio? Sure he made you. Made you suck him off that morning, paid you with a fifty and then *made* you come back that night."

"He threatened me." Kip's voice cracks. "He raped me."

"Sure. Raped you. Like you came walking into his room backwards with your pants around your ankles, squatted down on his dick, and he raped you." Fagan circles him, staring him up and down, swirling the glass. "Turn around and face me."

Kip turns—

And instantly finds himself splayed on the carpet, knocked against the sofa. His face is on fire, stinging as if he had run headlong into a nest of hornets. When Fagan slaps, it hurts like hell.

The big man towers over him. He steps on Kip's bare feet, one at a time. Kip squeals and draws them back. Fagan steps closer, planting his foot squarely onto Kip's crotch.

Fagan looks down and shakes his head. "You're not very bright, are you, kid? I know your type. Good for fucking and not much else. I told you not to lie to me." The pressure increases. Kip squirms against the sofa, unable to budge, his balls pinned to the floor. "And I told you to call me sir, didn't I? Answer me, punk."

More pressure. Kip is close to crying. His voice squeaks. "Yes, sir."

Fagan nods. "Better." The pressure eases. Beneath the sole of his shoe, Kip's cock is bone-hard.

Kip sniffles. Wipes his nose. Looks furtively up to Fagan's face, looming far and indistinct above him, then down. His gaze settles on the crotch of Fagan's loose, baggy dress slacks. Kip raises his eyebrows. Widens his eyes.

Only inches from his face—close enough to turn him cross-eyed. So close, so obvious, no one could possibly miss it.

Karl Fagan has a big one.

Kip stares at the bulging folds of cloth that hang from the man's crotch, full and heavy like lemons in a sack—like a baby's arm cradled in a sling. Kip can smell it, wafting from Fagan's crotch. The odor of sex. The powerful musk generated by a vast expanse of cockflesh and balls. The smell is a narcotic. Kip forgets his fear.

Three months since Zorio. Three months since Kip has been fed. Kip has been hungry the whole time, not even aware of how hungry he was. Without thinking, he wets his lips and opens his mouth in a slack-jawed sigh. He closes his eyes and leans forward. His lips graze the fine, smooth fabric of Fagan's slacks, just above the straining zipper. The odor is overwhelming. Kip can feel the heat—

And then the pressure at his crotch is gone. The

Kip

heat and smell recede. Kip is kissing empty air, and somewhere above him Fagan is laughing.

Fagan walks to the bar, sets his glass on the counter with a bang. He reaches for the bottle of whiskey and pours another.

"You see, Kip, I have my own private file on you—started it the night they wheeled in Zorio's corpse. Oh, you were the talk of the station, believe me. For days. Weeks. It still hasn't stopped. There's not a cop in this town, and not a cop's buddy, and not one of *their* buddies who haven't heard the story—the one about the big-dicked gangster and the faggot bellboy who got caught with his pants down. You're a celebrity, kid. The most talked about cocksucker in town."

Fagan downs the glass, then sets it carelessly aside. "*You should have seen it*—that's what they all keep saying. You had to be there. That naked blond kid, pretty as a girl, standing there with Zorio's dick up his rear end, eyes as big as saucers, quivering like a fish on a hook—and then he starts coming, just like that, not even touching himself, squirting his load for the whole world to see. And when the guns went off and Zorio came sliding out of blondie's ass—goddamn, you never saw such a piece of dago dick. Like a fuckin' baseball bat ... That's what they all say, the guys who were there."

Fagan cocks his head. "They right, kid? Like a baseball bat?" Fagan smirks. "You like 'em big, Kip? Really big?" He slides his hands into his pants pockets, pulling the fabric taut across his crotch—as if the lump there were not already conspicuous enough. "Big enough to choke you? Big enough to split your tight little boycunt wide open?"

Kip stares, the hunger in his eyes as blatant as the bulge at Fagan's crotch. Fagan shakes his head in disgust. He begins to pace, back and forth, his steps defining an arc with Kip crouching at its center.

"So I kept hearing the stories, about this cute little blond Zorio was screwing when they broke in on him. Not to mention the stuff they found—handcuffs, enema bag. Wire coat hanger. Kinky stuff. I said to myself: this kid was no virgin off the street. This kid was a pro. I smelled vice.

"So I got permission to do a little interrogation. Zorio's partner, Battaglia. He was already pretty ragged by the time I got to him. No kid gloves for that dago. Battaglia's a worm, a nobody. At his age, taking orders from a young guy like Zorio—got no bargaining power, doesn't know shit. So they let me do whatever I wanted. He had plenty to say about you, Kip."

Fagan curls his lip in a sneer. "Imagine a fat slob like that, sticking his dick inside a pretty thing like you. Wallowing all over you while he squirts his come up your butt. I guess if it's big enough you don't much care what it's attached to, do you, Kip?"

Kip lowers his eyes and says nothing.

"You know, Kip, I don't really mind that you take it up the ass. I don't give a damn if you get down on your knees for every fat, balding businessman from here to Omaha. It's your mouth, Kip. It's your ass. But when you start selling it, that's my business. Because you're in my territory. And nobody sells ass in my territory without Karl Fagan's explicit permission. You understand?"

Kip bites his lip, afraid to speak.

Fagan laughs and shakes his head. He walks to the bar and fixes another drink. "Like I said, you're not very smart, are you? No brain, no balls. Hardly got a dick between your legs, from what I hear. Just another dumb blond not worth a damn except for a couple

Kip

of hot, tight holes where a man can sink his dick. Worthless. Piece of trash." Fagan swallows from the glass and looks thoughtful. "Let me put it in one-syllable words, Kip. You're a whore. Max is your pimp. I'm vice. You want to work in this town, you work *through* me, understand? You make sure I stay happy. Or else I could make you very, very unhappy. Make you hurt, Kip. Make you cry. Make you bleed if I have to. Let me show you something."

Fagan reaches for his coat, slides his hand into the inner breast pocket. He stands in front of Kip, looming directly above him. "You ever seen one of these?"

Kip looks up. The blackjack is strapped to Fagan's wrist, the leather loops crisscrossing the back of his hand. The shaft hangs loosely from his fist at crotch level, like a big flaccid dick. Fagan slaps it against the palm of his hand with a hard, meaty crack.

"This is what I used on Leo Battaglia. A big guy like that—nothing but a pussy, if you got the right tool. Willing to talk in two minutes flat. *Begging* me to let him talk. Only I couldn't let him off that easy. Not enough fun in two measly minutes. I must have worked that bastard over for two solid hours."

Fagan cracks the blackjack against his palm. Kip jerks. Fagan rubs the blunt tip against Kip's cheek.

"Hit a guy in the nuts with this thing about twenty times—you better believe he'll start talking. I bet I could make you talk, too, Kip. I bet I could make you say just about anything I wanted to hear."

Kip shivers, the touch of the blackjack turning his cheek to gooseflesh. "Please. Please, sir. What do you want from me?"

Fagan narrows his eyes and croons. "That's not bad, Kip. Not bad for starters. What do I want? A piece of your ass—the piece that belongs to me. My fair share.

You understand, punk? You've been operating without Karl Fagan's permission. Selling that sweet little boypussy of yours behind my back. Keeping all the green for yourself. That's just not allowed."

Kip hangs his head. "I didn't know."

"Ignorance is no excuse. But don't worry. We'll work it out." Fagan reaches down, seizes Kip by the jaw and pulls him to his toes. "It's mainly your Uncle Max I'm mad at. Sonofabitch—pimping behind my back."

Kip closes his eyes. Max is innocent, but Fagan will not listen.

"So it's Uncle Max who's gonna feel the real heat. But I'm not letting you off the hook completely. No way, punk. You're still gonna get your punishment."

Kip is swallowed by prickly heat. His whole body blushes a furious red to match the skimpy kimono.

Fagan smiles. "Been a while since I've had a piece of boyass on my beat. Mostly bitches in my territory. Oh, I get a few boys now and then, selling their cracks right alongside the real thing, but they seem to come and go. Usually something bad happens to 'em. Doesn't matter. They're all girls to me. Looks like you're gonna join the family, Kip. Looks like you're gonna be one of Fagan's girls from now on. What do you say?"

Kip makes no answer. Fagan is very close, surrounding him, looming over him, blocking out everything else. Fagan's hand is on his thigh, caressing the taut, naked flesh, sliding up to the black panties, cupping Kip's ass, pulling him close. Fagan's voice is deep and breathy and moist against Kip's face, scented with whiskey.

"The girls on my beat, they got a nickname for me. Use it behind my back. You know what they call me, baby?"

Kip shakes his head.

"They call me the Punisher." Fagan caresses Kip's mouth with the blackjack, tracing the smooth tip against his lips. He fondles the boy's ass. His middle finger wriggles into the crack. His crotch presses against Kip's groin. "And I got a nickname for them. Call 'em my little squealers. You know why?" Kip is too frightened to answer. Fagan prompts him by gently batting the blackjack against his cheek—a light tap, just enough to give him a taste of the thing's power. Hard and heavy as a brick.

"No, sir—why do you call them ... your little squealers?"

Fagan laughs softly. "Take any one of my girls, put us alone in a room with a lock on the door, and I guarantee I'll have her squealing like a pig in two minutes flat. One way or another." Fagan pushes the end of the blackjack against Kip's mouth, forcing it open. He slips an inch inside, then another, watching the boy's lips open in a perfect **O**. "I bet I could make you squeal, too, Kip. I bet I could have a lot of fun doing it. I think maybe I will."

Fagan grins. He pulls the blackjack from Kip's mouth with a pop and rubs it wet and slick over the boy's cheeks. His finger caresses Kip's hole through the sheer black panties. His cock throbs, huge and confined, like a living animal trapped between them. "So where do you like it best, Kip? In your mouth—or up your ass? Huh? Tell me where you like it best."

"Please—" Kip struggles, but Fagan only tightens his grip.

"Tell me." Fagan crushes him.

"In my—up my ass ... I guess ... *oh!*"

There is a sudden, deafening banging at the door, only inches away—Kip almost jumps out of his skin, but Fagan holds him tight. Kip swings his head wildly from Fagan's face to the door and back. Fagan seems undisturbed by the interruption, as if he expected it. His only reaction is a thin smile.

"Looks like we've got company, baby. Don't worry about it—just one of my boys from vice, dropping by to pick me up. You ready to go for a little ride, Kip?"

The banging at the door continues. Kip tries again to break away from Fagan's embrace, but the big man holds him tight. One viselike hand grips his neck. The other cradles his bottom. The finger stroking his crack suddenly wriggles inside the sheer black panties and makes contact with the nude, moist ring of his asshole. Kip lets out a gasp—and then another. In the blink of an eye, Fagan's middle finger is knuckle-deep inside him. Kip goes rigid. Fagan smiles. He yells from the corner of his mouth. "Come on in, Pike!"

The door opens and shuts. Behind him, Kip hears a low whistle. "Shit, boss. Looks like you've hooked yourself a live one."

Kip blushes. He breaks out in a cold sweat. The presence of the unseen intruder changes everything. His will to resist evaporates, replaced by shame, fear, excitement. Instead of trying to break away, he presses his body against Fagan's, instinctively seeking shelter, a place to hide.

Fagan is impassive, like a man made of stone. Only his finger moves, rudely stroking Kip's prostate. He feels the change in the boy, the sudden melting submission; but now, instead of crushing him tight, Fagan pushes Kip away, spinning him around to face the newcomer. He shoves him forward, like a boy on a spit, a toy impaled on his middle finger.

"What do you think, Pike?"

Kip glances up, only for an instant, just enough to

Kip

see the man looking him up and down and slowly nodding.

"Like I said, boss, live bait. Hot stuff. Just like all the guys at the station made him out, real blond and pretty. Big titties ..."

"And lousy manners. Come on, Kippy, is this the way Uncle Max taught you to greet a stranger? Say hello to my associate, Mr. Pike."

Even as he speaks, Fagan keeps churning his middle finger inside the boy's rectum, stoking him, poking him, loosening him up. Turning his insides to jelly. Kip's legs wobble. His breath is ragged. His face burns hotter than ever. He can hardly think. A second finger begins to poke at the lips of his ass, and Fagan's voice returns, warm and moist in his ear.

"Go ahead, bitch, say hello and do it right. Or do you want me to *make* you?"

"Please—" Kip shakes his head. Fagan's forefinger slides in alongside the other, stretching his hole, kneading hard against his prostate. "Oh, please—" He manages to raise his head. Pike is dressed like Fagan, in a dark, conservative suit. Wavy jet-black hair, cut short and shiny with grease. A younger man than Fagan, barely older than Kip. The baby-face type, big and brawny like a football player. Sparkly eyes and sweet, pouty lips, with a hint of something wicked beneath his wholesome good looks.

"Hello—" Kip's voice breaks. He clears his throat. "Hello, Mr. Pike."

Pike snorts. "Talks like a sissy."

"That's 'cause he is a sissy. Aren't you, Kip?" Fagan pinches a sensitive spot deep in the boy's ass, sending a jolt up Kip's spine. Kip yelps and shudders and does a spastic little dance.

"Yes, sir!"

The two men laugh.

"Go ahead, Pike, get to work. The old queen's bedroom is down that hallway. Start there."

Pike nods. He flashes a final leer that runs like a live wire up and down Kip's shivering body, then disappears into Max's bedroom. A moment later there's a loud bang and the sound of shattered glass.

"What—what's he doing?" Kip gives a start, but Fagan curls his fingers tightly, using them like a hook to hold the boy in place.

"Just a standard search."

"For what?"

"You talk too much, baby." Fagan pulls him backward, pressing Kip's shoulders to his big chest, grabbing his mouth and twisting it around to cover it with a kiss. The man's tongue slides deep into Kip's mouth and tickles the back of his throat. His fingers stoke in and out of the boy's hole, sliding in knuckle-deep, then pulling out to nip and pinch at the tender lips. He pulls at the thin strip of fabric that rides above the boy's asshole, draws it back like a rubber band and snaps it against the puckered hole. He catches Kip's squeal in his mouth and breathes it back into Kip's lungs, and in the same instant slips his fingers back inside—first one finger, then two. Then a third.

Fagan breaks the kiss. Kip groans, then staggers forward, batting his eyes open. Fagan pushes him toward his bedroom.

Kip is forced to stagger bowlegged, straddling the fingers up his ass. He walks in a daze, then comes to a sudden halt as Fagan reels him back, using his hand as a hook. Fagan forces him onto his toes, hoisting him upward. The room spins before him. The snow-white drapes, drawn against the midday sun, filling the room with warm, soft light. The rumpled satin sheets, still moist with his sweat. The dresser, and the mirror above it—

Kip

Kip sees himself and starts. His shiny blond hair is rumpled from sleep, his head thrown back, eyes narrowed, lips parted. The skimpy red silk kimono lies open below his throat, its sash loosened at his waist, showing off the hard cleavage of his chest and the smooth inner curve of each big, smooth pectoral; his skin is shiny with sweat, glistening in the light. Fagan towers behind him in the mirror, his face above Kip's, smirking. For an instant their eyes meet, then Kip looks away.

"You see, Kip, we have to search your room, too."

"But—what for?"

"Who knows what you and Uncle Max are up to? A whore and his pimp—could be just about anything. Drugs. Kiddie porn. Snuff movies. Secret diaries. Stuff that could give me and my boys a—well, let's say an additional advantage in dealing with a piece of trash like your Uncle Max. Well, well. Wonder what's in here?"

In the mirror, Kip follows Fagan's gaze to the small drawer in the middle of the dresser, slightly open with a bit of shiny fabric hanging over the edge. Open, because Kip reached inside accidentally when he was getting dressed. The drawer where he keeps the panties he's now wearing, the ones he grabbed by mistake in his sleepy stupor, the panties he wore for Vince Zorio—and now for Karl Fagan. The drawer where he keeps his secret things, things he doesn't even share with Max—

Kip's heart begins to pound in his chest. Fagan feels it in the boy's guts, a sudden clenching and a throbbing vein in the sleek flesh beneath his buried fingers. Kip reaches to close the drawer. Fagan slaps his hand aside and laughs softly.

"What's the matter, Kip? Something in there you don't want me to see?"

"No, please—"

"Shut up, punk. Now reach down there like a good little boy and show me what you're hiding." Fagan wedges a fold of flesh between his probing fingers and gives Kip another hard pinch deep inside. *"Do it."*

A gasp of pain. A whimper of defeat. Then Kip reaches out, bending slightly, impaling himself even deeper onto Fagan's stroking fingers. His own hands tremble as he slides them over the edge of the drawer and slowly opens it for Fagan's inspection.

Fagan chuckles. "Muscles, huh? You like 'em big all over, don't you, Kip?" He reaches out and picks up the first magazine in the stack. The cover shows a young bodybuilder with a bleached blond crew cut, head bowed and hands clenched behind his back, shaved and oiled and lit starkly from above. Fagan stares at it for an instant, then tosses it aside. He picks up each of the magazines in the stack below and does the same, one by one, until the carpet is littered with scattered images of musclemen posing in skimpy posing straps.

As Fagan picks up the last magazine, Kip blushes a deeper shade of red. He tries to shut the drawer again, but Fagan uses the magazine to bat his hands away.

"Not so quick, sweetheart. Looks like your little trousseau is just starting to get interesting. Looks like maybe you picked up a few nasty habits from the late Mr. Zorio."

Fagan picks up the items one by one, studying each in turn before tossing it to the floor. He slaps the leather dog collar against Kip's nipples and belly, making him flinch. He dangles the matching chain against the boy's naked skin, turning it to gooseflesh. He rubs the thick rubber dildo up Kip's belly to his throat, over his chin to his lips, pushing it into his mouth for a moment before tossing it aside. He toys with the wooden clothespins, dangling them from Kip's erect nipples, feeling the boy's hole clench around his fingers as he yanks them off.

Then he finds the thing that Kip has been dreading most. A small square of newsprint, already beginning to turn yellow, tucked inside an envelope covered with greasy fingerprints. Clipped from the front page of the morning paper, the day after the shooting at the hotel. Two side-by-side portraits, one straight-on and the other a profile, above the headline: NOTORIOUS HIT MAN SLAIN BY POLICE. Even in mug shots, Vince Zorio was damned good looking.

Kip gives a shudder and instinctively snatches at the bit of newsprint. Fagan is too quick for him.

"Yeah, that's Zorio all right. Looking about as happy as the last time I saw him, stretched out on a slab in the morgue. I thought you told me Zorio raped you, Kippy, made you bend over against your will. So why the souvenir, stuck in here with all your sex toys? Funny thing, ain't it—looks like your fingers are always greasy whenever you go to pull his picture out of that little envelope. And so many fingerprints—must be something you do pretty often."

Kip blushes furiously and looks away. Fagan waves the clipping before his face. "Look at it, punk. I said *look at it*."

Kip swallows hard and stares at the yellowing pictures, so close he turns cross-eyed. His heart speeds up—Fagan can feel the pulse in his bowels. His eyes become glazed; he licks his bottom lip to catch a sudden gush of spittle. His hole begins to twitch and loosen and then to spread wide open, as if he were trying to swallow Fagan's entire hand. Just from looking at a couple of grainy mug shots of Vince Zorio.

"You little cunt," Fagan whispers. He slowly crumples the clipping in his fist, destroying it. Kip gives a gasp and a start, but Fagan holds him in place.

"Yo, boss. Hope I'm not interrupting a special moment."

Fagan and Kip both turn with a jerk. Pike is lounging in the doorway, arms crossed, a smirk on his pretty-boy face.

Fagan's face goes blank for an instant. Then he turns back to Kip, smiling. He tosses the crumpled clipping onto the floor along with the rest of Kip's secrets. "Find anything?"

"Nada, boss. All I know is the old queen likes opera posters and tacky wallpaper. Must like looking at himself, too. Musta been a dozen mirrors in his bedroom. Or maybe he likes the mirrors for when he screws the kid, huh?" Pike flicks his eyes up and down Kip's body and purses his lips.

"So get to work in here. I want this room ripped apart. And as for you, pussyboy—" Fagan pulls his fingers from Kip's rectum with a squelching pop and gives the boy's gaping hole a hard, open-handed swat. "Lean over the bed. Legs spread, hands on the mattress, ass up. Move it!"

Kip remains in place, his eyes shut, afraid to move, listening to the sound of his room being torn apart. Broken glass. The sharp clinking of clothes hangers racked together, the soft crash of clothing thrown to the floor. The banging of drawers opened and slammed, the explosion of contents spilled onto the already cluttered floor.

"Find anything, Pike?"

"Nothing, boss. But have you had a look at the kid's underwear? Uncle Max sure likes to dress him up, huh? Sorta like his own personal little Ken doll."

"Except I never saw Ken wearing black lace panties."

Both men snort with laughter.

"This is getting us nowhere. Come on, Pike. Time to clear out. We can always plant something later if we need to."

"Sure thing, boss."

In the sudden silence, Kip goes rigid. Ever since Fagan forced him to bend over the bed—legs spread, ass up, his panties peeled down to bare his cheeks—he's been waiting for this moment, dreading it. Of course, Fagan intends to rape him. So does Pike. Kip hears them draw closer. He breaks into a cold sweat.

"What do you think, Pike? Think little Kippy here is ready?"

Pike laughs. "Sure, why not?"

Fagan is close beside him, his voice warm and moist in Kip's ear. "Hey, kiddo. It's not what you think. I'm not going to fuck you. Not yet. I told you we were going for a little ride, didn't I? Well, now it's time. Only you can't go out like this, can you? Not with your pussy gaping wide open. Thinking about Zorio's got your hole *too* loose. I'm gonna stop it up for you."

"Hey, boss, how about using this?" Pike grins and holds up the dildo. The pliant rubber flops back and forth above his fist.

"Kid stuff," Fagan says. "I got something better."

Something strikes the mattress, two inches from Kip's nose. His eyes pop wide open. His asshole clenches shut. "No. No, please—"

Fagan lifts the blackjack and slaps it hard and meaty against the palm of his hand. "What's the matter, Kippy? You don't want my blackjack up your cunt?" He rubs the hard leather against Kip's crack.

AARON TRAVIS

"Funny thing—neither did Leo Battaglia. I told you about interrogating Leo. Talk about squealers. Blubbered like a baby when I rammed this thing up his butthole. Know what else I put up his ass?" Fagan laughs. "Yeah, it's pretty sickening, ain't it, just the idea of porking his big fat ass. But I figured there was no better way to put that worm in his place. Told him he might as well get used to it—there'd be plenty more cock for a wimp like him, where he was headed. I wonder if your precious Zorio ever fucked him, some night when they were both really hard-up? What do you think, Kip? Think I should fuck your pussy, the way I fucked old Leo?"

Fagan strokes the blackjack up and down Kip's crack, poking at his hole. "Hey, Pike. Bring me that jar of Vaseline from the kid's dresser...."

Kip stands in the center of the room, hands at his sides, his face a flaming red, his body drenched with sweat. The blackjack feels enormous up his ass, like a snake coiled in his guts, a python lodged inside him. The skimpy bottom panel of his panties wasn't enough to hold it in place; Fagan had Pike bring some electrical tape from the utility room.

"He's still not ready to go out, boss."

"What do you mean?"

"His feet. Gotta have something on his feet. But hey"—Pike snaps his fingers—"I saw just the thing. In his closet."

Pike steps into the walk-in. An instant later he returns with a pair of black patent-leather shoes. Fagan takes them in one hand, nods, and drops them at Kip's feet. "Put on your shoes, bitch."

Kip looks down and groans. Somehow, he knew what Pike would bring. The mail-order shoes that Max bought him, the ones he wears around the house sometimes, only because he knows that Max like to see him in them. A pair of open-toed high platform shoes; not exactly high heels, but pitched forward enough to tilt his arches, flex his calves, and give a lift to his buttocks. He steps into them and grows three inches.

"Go ahead, Kip. Walk into the living room."

Kip takes a faltering step, then another, listening to the men laugh behind him. The slip-on shoes have no straps; to keep them on, he has to maintain a stilted, staggering gait. The look is unnatural, awkward, strangely erotic; like a geisha with stunted little-girl feet, or a boy with his ankles hobbled. It's even harder to walk with the blackjack up his ass.

"I think we're finally ready," Fagan says. "What do you say, Kippy? Shall we go say hello to your Uncle Max?"

The platform shoes make a loud clack against the pavement. The rhythm is broken, syncopated, thrown off by Kip's staggering gait. Kip feels feverish and chilled by turns, transparent and slightly unreal, as if he's trapped in a dream, a nightmare. He has never felt more humiliated or ashamed in his life. His cock is hard as stone.

It all happened so quickly, he still can hardly believe that any of it is real. Pike opened the door. Fagan shoved him forward. And then he was in the hallway outside the apartment, with no money, no keys, and suddenly a pair of handcuffs around his wrists. "Standard procedure," Fagan had purred. "For your own protection," Pike smirked. "We wouldn't want you to hurt yourself."

The gray-haired woman across the hall opened her door a few inches—she must have heard the racket they'd made during the search. Her eyes grew wide.

The door opened another few inches. "Police," Fagan growled, flashing his badge. "Go on about your business, lady." In half an hour the whole building would know.

They goosed him in the elevator, pinching his buttocks, pushing against the stump of the blackjack to make sure it was still in place. The ride down fourteen stories had never seemed longer. A tenant joined them on the tenth floor. Another on the seventh. Two more on the third. At each stop, Fagan flashed his badge in silence, and the little elevator was filled with a strained embarrassment. Kip thought he would die.

Now he walks down the crowded sidewalk, his heart pounding so hard that it drowns out the blare of traffic. With no arms for balance, he trips in his platform shoes. Fagan catches his shoulder and rights him. Pike cops a feel of his thigh, edging his fingertips along the hem of Kip's panties.

Kip walks on. In his skimpy silk robe. In his fuck-me panties and high heels, handcuffed, with the blackjack throbbing in his asshole. Not a short walk—the car is only a half-block away, but Fagan takes a long, circuitous route, making sure Kip is seen by the lunchtime mob on the sidewalks.

The sash about his waist loosens. He can't retie it. The robe falls open. Kip walks with his nipples erect and his little cock pushing hard against the thin fabric of his panties for all the world to gawk at. Men stare. Women laugh. An old wino glares at him and spits on the pavement. A mother with two little boys pushes their faces against her skirts to keep them from seeing. A businessman with a *Wall Street Journal* can't hide the sudden mask of lust that contorts his face; even after they pass, Kip can still feel the man's eyes on him, like a burning hand against his jiggling cheeks. A teamster unloading a truck spots the handcuffs and turns a thumbs-up. "Good for you guys—that's what you cops oughta be doing, getting that kind of trash off the street!"

The warehouse is in a part of town Kip has never been to before, somewhere on the waterfront. He can hear the low thudding horns and whistles of ships and the screeching of seagulls; but the sounds are echoey and vague, muffled by the high concrete walls that surround the deserted little parking lot.

Fagan hustles him out of the back seat and shoves him toward a loading ramp. Broken glass crunches underfoot. Ancient garbage lies in windswept banks against the walls. Kip ascends the ramp. His high heels catch on the wooden slats. Fagan grips his arm to keep him moving, squeezing hard enough to leave bruises.

They enter the anteroom of the old warehouse. Shattered glass, naked wires, dust and ashes everywhere. Plaster fallen from the walls in chunks, abandoned filing cabinets. There's a sudden rustling in one corner—a rat the size of a cat scurries across the floor. Its tail whips against Kip's toes. He lets out a stifled yelp. Fagan and Pike only laugh, and push him through the next portal.

They step into the big main room, two stories high. Most of the skylights and the big windows near the ceiling are covered with black paint. A few, streaked with whitewash, admit a sickly bleached light. Much of the big room lies in shadow, even in the middle of the day. At first the cavernous room seems deserted, until Kip hears a hard slap followed by a gasp. He turns his head and sees them at the far corner of the room, almost swallowed by darkness. Two men—one standing, one sitting—beneath a cone of harsh white light cast by a hooded bulb that hangs on a long wire from the ceiling.

Fagan and Pike each give him a hard shove. Kip staggers toward the light, growing more frightened with each awkward step.

The man standing beneath the light is huge, with enough muscle and fat for two men. He suddenly stops what he's doing and turns toward them. He wears a sweat-stained undershirt and a baggy pair of black trousers held up by suspenders. His iron gray hair is cut in a severe flattop. His features are crude and jowly, like an old marine sergeant gone to seed. He gives a nod to Fagan and Pike, then stares at Kip, curls his upper lip, and fondles the blackjack in his hand. Kip meets his eyes, but only for an instant. He had thought that no man could be more frightening than Karl Fagan. He was wrong.

The other man remains seated as they approach. He has no choice. His ankles are tied to the chair legs, his arms pulled behind the seat back and handcuffed. His mouth is covered by a wide strip of silver tape. The man wears only a grimy pair of underwear, stained yellow at the crotch where he's wet himself. Compared to the giant, he seems very small, and his body looks revoltingly soft and doughy, unredeemed by any muscle. Judging from the bruises on his pasty white flesh, the giant has been working him over for quite some time. His head hangs down, his chin rests against his chest, but he doesn't sleep. His eyelids flicker as they approach. His seedy little mustache gives a twitch. Uncle Max is not a pretty sight.

Fagan breathes in Kip's ear. "So that's the stud you give it to every night, huh, baby? A pretty sorry sight. Maybe you'd like to take his place?"

Kip shudders. Fagan steps away, into the light. "How's it going, Lugar?"

Kip

"No problems, boss." The giant slaps the black-jack against his palm and lets out a fart, all the while staring Kip up and down.

What happens next is so sudden and shocking that it seems hardly possible to Kip, as if he has descended into a deeper, darker circle of nightmares. The harsh light and shadows, the glint off Fagan's gold ring as he lifts his open hand, the melting grin on Lugar's face—all become weirdly surreal as Fagan steps forward in slow motion and begins to slap Max back and forth, back and forth, making his head ricochet like a pinball from shoulder to shoulder. Slapping so long that the sight becomes ludicrous, almost comic. At least the cops think so. Pike laughs. Lugar giggles.

Without missing a beat, Fagan raises his foot and plants it in Max's crotch, so hard he knocks the chair over with a crash. Max lies on his side, whimpering and squealing behind his gag. Narrowing his eyes as if to pretend he's unconscious, shooting frightened little glances up at Fagan, who stalks him in a slow circle, looking down his nose and shaking his head.

"Fucking pimp," Fagan mutters. He gives Max a swift kick in the belly, then picks him up by a fistful of hair, chair and all, and sets him down on the floor. The silver tape muffles his screams. Kip blinks in amazement.

Fagan slaps his hands together, dusting them off, and returns to Kip. Smiling. Breathing evenly. As if nothing had happened. He steps behind Kip, unlocks the handcuffs, and slips them into his coat pocket.

Kip looks over his shoulder in surprise, then down at his wrists. He rubs the chafed skin, wincing as the circulation returns. He glances toward Max. For an instant their eyes meet—and Kip realizes that Max is only now aware of his presence. The look on his uncle's bruised and mottled face is almost more frightening than anything else, because it's so strange. Hatred, shame, fear, desire ...

Then Fagan's hands are on Kip's thighs, gliding up his hips, circling his belly, cupping his big, smooth swimmer's pecs from behind. Feeling him up while Max watches. Nibbling his ear and plucking at his nipples.

"You look pretty in your little red kimono, Kip. Real pretty. You know, I've been to Japan. All over the East. Marines. MP in Yokohama. Busted plenty of whores there. Or busted their cunts, anyway." He chuckles. "Gook girls don't like 'em big. You know that? Says it hurts 'em inside. Those whores took off like rabbits whenever they saw me coming. You wanna know why?"

Kip knows. Kip can feel it, throbbing through Fagan's trousers, nudging warm and thick against the crack of his ass.

Fagan steps back. He pulls the kimono open from behind, sliding it over Kip's shoulders. The silk grazes light as a sigh over his flesh and flutters shimmering to the floor. Fagan draws close again, pressing against his backside. "There. Now you look like a genuine Yokohama slut, showing off those pretty tits. Except maybe for the panties. Yeah, no Yokohama whore would wear a pair of panties, not alone in a room with three men. Might get in the way of any dick that might happen to want inside one of her holes. Be a good little girl, Kip. Give us a show. Take off your panties."

Kip swallows hard. He can feel them looking. Pike. Lugar. Max. All of them waiting. Fagan's cock throbs against his ass. Fagan's breath is hot against his neck. He reaches down and slips his hands inside the briefs. He bends and slides them over his hips.

His hard-on pokes up against his belly. The panties slip over his thighs and flutter to his ankles.

Kip begins to straighten. Fagan stops him. "Uh-uh. Stay just like that."

Kip is suddenly dizzy from the blood rushing to his head. He drops his hands to the floor, keeps his feet spread and his legs straight, hoisting his ass up high. Fagan grunts in approval. Pike sucks in his breath, letting it out in a long *Ooooooo*. In the background, Kip hears a constant spanking—Lugar slapping the blackjack against his palm. And an odd, strangled, blubbering noise. Uncle Max is crying like a baby.

Fagan's hands are cool and smooth against his naked ass. "Pussyboy. Isn't that what Zorio called you? Mmmm. Usually I like my pussy between a woman's legs, but I gotta admit—I think I see what got Zorio so turned on." He rips off the electrical tape. Kip gasps, then moans as Fagan's blackjack oozes slowly from his rectum, inch by inch, until it falls to the floor with a bang. Uncle Max blubbers louder than ever.

Fagan breathes out a sigh of pure lust. He unzips his trousers. "Hey, Pike, you bring that Vaseline from little Kippy's bedroom? No, never mind—I think he's greased up enough already...."

Karl Fagan has a very big cock. Bigger than Max's. Bigger than Zorio's. Probably ten times bigger than Kip's little weenie, jabbing like a finger against his belly with each cruel thrust from behind, rock-hard in spite of the suffering in his bowels.

Big. Thick. Kip still hasn't seen it, but he's felt it—every inch, forced full length up his ass, over and over. Fagan is not a gentle man. Fagan fucks hard. Fagan is cruel, demanding, relentless. Kip has never felt anything like it. Like being punched in the belly over and over, only deep inside. No wonder the whores in Yokohama hated Fagan so much. No wonder the girls on his beat call him the Punisher.

And they're my little squealers, Fagan had said. Kip started squealing before the thing was even halfway in. Squealing, struggling, running for his life. He managed to pull himself off the horn of Fagan's cock and made for the door, no idea of where he was going, desperate to get away from the monster Fagan was trying to put inside him. He took three steps before he tripped over the panties around his ankles and fell flat on his face. Fagan only laughed and picked up him and started all over again....

That was over half an hour ago. Or days, or weeks, as far as Kip can tell. He's long since surrendered to the thing between Fagan's legs. There's even a kind of pleasure in the ordeal, there must be—his own hard cock is the proof. Still, every time Fagan grinds his hips and corkscrews his cock as deep as it can reach, Kip throws back his head and lets out a little squeal. He can't help it.

Behind him, Fagan laughs. "What's the matter, pussyboy? I thought you liked 'em big." He pulls back, then slams forward. Kip throws back his head and squeals.

"Tight as a twelve-year-old virgin," Fagan mutters. "Looks like Uncle Max has been falling down on the job. Working in the kitchen when he should've been porking your hole twice a night." He digs his fingers into the buttery flesh of Kip's thighs and rocks him forward and back, pushing until the boy's hole smooches the tip of his cock like puckered lips, then yanking him back until he's cruelly impaled on the huge cock, jerking and squealing like a pig.

"Yeah, I know what you like. Had a look at Zorio, the night they brought him in. Died with a fucking

Kip

hard-on, still greasy from screwing your cunt. Stayed that way—laid out on the slab as stiff as a board, with a boner to match." Fagan slams it home. Kip squeals. "Hung like a fucking donkey, wasn't he, Kip? You must've really gone to town on that one. Almost as big as the dick you got up your pussy right now …"

Suddenly Fagan's cock swells even larger. The vice cop is ready to come.

Kip feels it expand in his ass, hears the sudden catch in Fagan's breath. He steels himself for the moment. He could almost come himself, never even touching his little weenie, just from the hugeness of it inside him. From the shame of bending over in a pair of high heels with his legs wide open and a big cock up his ass. From the humiliation of being used while the others watch, Pike and Lugar laughing and groping themselves, blubbering Uncle Max. From the mere mention of Zorio's name, and the memory of the last time he stood nude and impaled before a roomful of men …

But Fagan isn't ready to shoot. Not yet. A loud, high pop echoes around the room, like a cork exploding from a bottle—or the sound of a huge cock abruptly wrenched from a tight, moist hole. Kip finds himself on the floor, the high heels twisting his ankles, both elbows smarting from the fall. For a moment he stares at the floor, dazed and confused, aware of nothing but the sudden, aching emptiness in his bowels. Then he turns and looks over his shoulder, at a cock too big to be real.

Somewhere far above, Fagan is smiling. Purring. Cock-proud. On the verge of coming. "Kiss me, Kip."

He clutches his cock with one hand, like a club. His pants are open, the zipper pulled down to let his big balls tumble free. The shaft is far too thick for his hand to encircle it. The taut, circumcised flesh glistens with a thick coating of rectal mucus. A bead of semen forms at the tip, falls, and hangs suspended.

"Kiss me, pussyboy."

Uncle Max is watching. Closer than Kip had realized. Fagan has practically been fucking him in Maxwell's face.

Pike and Lugar draw closer. Groping themselves. Pike draws back his pretty-boy lips in a sneer. Lugar giggles and slaps the blackjack against his thigh.

"Come on, cuntlips. Give daddy a kiss."

The thing is huge, a vast expanse of nude, glistening meat. A cuntbuster, ass splitter, throat wrecker. A truncheon to keep bad girls in line. Big enough to turn even big bad Leo into just another squealer. It looms even larger as Kip draws nearer on his hands and knees. The odor is overwhelming. He can smell himself on Fagan's cock. His asshole twinges, then abruptly goes slack, letting out a long, fluttering fart. The men all laugh—Kip imagines even Max is laughing, behind his gag. Above the mocking laughter, he hears a strange whimpering—and realizes it comes from his own throat. From a spot deep inside that needs to be filled by Fagan's cock. Filled and fucked the way his asshole was fucked.

Kip opens wide and presses his mouth to the blunt tip. So massive, his lips could never hope to encompass the whole thing. A kiss is the most he can manage, a gaping, open-mouthed kiss, lips pressed to cock like a hungry leech as Fagan groans above him and with a single pulse fills his mouth with slippery warm semen, followed by jet after powerful jet of the strong, musky stuff, so much his cheeks are bloated with it, pumping so hard and fast it backflushes in his throat, bursts from the seal of his straining lips and dribbles like slag down his chin, whitewashing his throat, running shiny and slick over the smooth, heavy flesh of his pectorals.

He reaches up to fondle Fagan's balls, cupping the suedelike flesh in his hands. The big testicles droop heavy as peaches against his palms, bouncing each time they contract to squirt a fresh dollop of semen into his mouth. He reaches higher, to caress Fagan's cock, to wrap his hands around the stalk and feel it throb with each new contraction.

But his hands close on empty air. Fagan steps back, drawing out of reach, breaking the seal of Kip's lips around his cockhead. Kip's mouth stays wide open. Big globs of semen drool from his lower lip and out the corners of his mouth.

Fagan sucks in a deep breath and grins. "Catching flies, kid?" His cock bounces in the air. A final jet of semen unfurls from the tip and lands with a splat, smack in the middle of Kip's gaping mouth.

Fagan stands for a long moment, hands at his sides, his cock slowly drooping, catching his breath. Then he pulls out a handkerchief and wipes his hands, stuffs his cock and balls back into his pants, and zips up. Finished with Kip, just as he finished with Max. Cool and collected, as if nothing had happened.

"Now, boss?" Pike leers at Kip. His cock is a long, stiff tube running down his pants leg. His voice is antsy.

"Steady, pal. You'll get yours. First I wanna make a couple more things clear to our guests here. You and Lugar untie the old man. And cover him up. He smells like pig sweat and piss."

Lugar tends to the handcuffs. Pike rips the tape from Max's mouth. The pain leaves him gasping and blind with tears. "You sonofabitch!" he screams. "Bastards! Who do you think you are? What have you done to him, what have you done to my little Kip—"

Fagan quiets him with a hard slap across the mouth. "Shut up, faggot. What've we done to the kid?" He snorts. "Nothing—compared to what happens next. It's not even dark yet." His lips compress into a grim smile as he turns to look down at Kip. The boy cringes nude on the floor, his face and chest shiny with come, his eyes wide with fear.

"What do you monsters want?" Max starts to blubber again. "Just tell me what you want."

"You fucked up, old queen. I'm not going to explain it again. You had to be punished, both of you. You've had yours. Kip's next. But first we talk about the future. We have to work out an arrangement that satisfies everybody, right? We expect future performance. We also expect back payments, with substantial penalties. You've been getting away with this pimp racket for a long time without even a whisper of green crossing my palm. Your account's way overdue. You might say that you and the kid are badly in arrears."

Pike and Lugar laugh as they hustle Max to his feet and start dressing him.

"From now on, I expect you and Kip to bring in so much a month—we'll come up with a hard figure later. I'm reasonable. All I ask for is my fair cut of Kip's ass, based on an average of selling it, say, five times a week. I don't think Kip'll find it too hard, getting five old geezers a week to stuff some cash up his pussy."

Max opens his mouth, but nothing comes out. Kip stares hard at the floor and turns his face away.

"And, of course, we expect fringe benefits. Like a crack at his hole, anytime I happen to be in the mood for some prime boycunt. Any time of the day or

Kip

night. Same for Pike and Lugar, naturally. And every now and then there may be a special friend I owe a favor to, some bigwig with a taste for blond ass and big, smooth tits; I expect Kip to bend over whenever and wherever he's told. By the way, I'll want my own key to your apartment. We'll have a copy cut on the drive back."

Max sways on his feet, looking clownish with his chef's jacket misbuttoned and his hair badly mussed and his face all red and purple. A big tear plunges from the corner of his eye and trickles down his cheek. "It's not fair," he whispers.

"Come on, old-timer." Fagan throws his arm around Max's shoulder. Max flinches, too weak to pull away. "I'll drive you home. You got a lot of cleaning up to do. The place is a mess."

"But what about … Kip?" Max looks over his shoulder, confused. Fagan keeps him walking.

"Kip will be home later tonight. Very late. Don't wait up."

Under the cone of light, Kip crawls backward like a spider, knocking over the chair, looking frantically for a place to hide. Pike and Lugar converge from different direction. "No! No! Uncle Max, help me! Stop them, Max! Uncle Max!"

Ashamed, defeated, Max doesn't even look back. He quickens his pace toward the exit.

Fagan pauses at the doorway. "Keep it piping hot while I'm gone, boys. See if you can't loosen up his jaw enough for me to use his throat when I get back."

"Sure thing, boss," Pike whispers, hurriedly unzipping his pants. But Fagan is already gone.

Much, much later—at five o'clock the next morning—there's a rattle at the the door to Uncle Max's apartment. The door opens to the sound of muffled voices. The door closes. The voices depart, leaving behind a shivering, hunched-over figure draped in a ratty old blanket.

Kip draws the blanket tight around his shoulders and peers about the room, illuminated only by moonlight. Amid the wreckage of overturned furniture, he spots Max sitting in silhouette before the big picture window across the room. So still and so quiet that Kip speaks his name in a hush of fear. "Max? Uncle Max?"

Max is not dead. Max is not even sleeping. He lets out a long, plaintive sigh.

Kip walks toward him, staggering. He trips and falls over a pile of scattered books. He stays on his hands and knees. Crawling is easier. The blanket catches on something. Kip crawls on, emerging naked as the blanket slips off his shoulders, his buttocks, his legs. His body gleams like burnished silver in the bright moonlight. Max lets out another sigh.

Kip is trembling. The soft light casts a haze about his body, camouflaging his condition. His bruised, puffy lips. The big hickey all across his chest and throat. The ruddy handprints on his ass. The bruises on his hips and thighs. His nipples swollen up to twice their normal size, protruding tender and erect from his heaving chest.

"Max," he whispers. "Forgive me, Max." His voice is scratchy and hoarse. Hard to talk, after the way they used his throat.

Max hangs his head. He raises one hand and waves it with a vague, dismissive motion. A gesture of helplessness, hopelessness, defeat.

Kip crawls closer. His eyes are shiny with tears. "No, Max, you have to forgive me. It's all my fault. I can't explain now, but we both know it was me. Things about me you never knew ..."

Kip

Max lifts his head. After a long moment, he nods comprehendingly. Max is no fool.

Kip crawls between the man's legs. Max wears a heavy cotton bathrobe, open below the waist. "Please, Uncle Max. I'm so sorry."

Max says nothing. He stares into the darkness.

"Please?" Kip peers up, unable to see his uncle's face. He bites his lip and lowers his eyes.

A moment later, Max lets out a strangled gasp as he feels himself engulfed by the boy's warm, sucking mouth. Despite himself, his cock almost instantly begins to grow and stiffen. Kip was always such a talented cocksucker. But Max is in no mood to forgive. He reaches down, intending to slap the boy away. Instead he draws back, fingers wet with tears.

Max leans back in the chair. The harder Kip sucks, the more the anger wells inside him, thinking of all the other men who have felt the same pleasure. Kip, doing it for money behind his back. Right in the hotel, making a fool of him before the staff. Deliberately putting himself in Vince Zorio's hands—and liking it. Bringing down Fagan's wrath. Max is damned lucky to be at home tonight, instead of in the hospital, or the morgue. And the pain and humiliation have only just begun. In a year's time, he'll probably be dead of ulcers or a heart attack, and it's all Kip's fault. The little whore should horsewhipped.

Kip pulls his mouth off. "Please," he sobs. "Please, Uncle Max."

No, Max will never forgive him. Not now. Not ever. He touches Kip's hair as if to stroke it, but instead pulls the boy's mouth roughly onto his cock, choking him with it. For a moment, at least, he can make the pain of Lugar's beating recede beneath the more immediate pleasure of fucking Kip's throat.

Aaron Travis

Fagan is right. The little slut is good for nothing else. A liar, a cheat, beneath contempt …

Who is he trying to fool? As he begins to come in Kip's throat, cradling the boy's face between his thighs in a tight, convulsive embrace, Max cannot stop himself from whispering, "Of course I forgive you, of course I do, oh Kip, how I love you, my good little boy…."

» THE BIG SHOT «

Kip sits naked and impaled on the hard wooden chair.

Wearing nothing but a dog collar.
In the center of the room.
Blindfolded.

He sits with his shoulders back, chest held high, head bowed. His hands are clasped together behind the chair. His legs are open, raised to tiptoe, quivering. His rectum is stretched wide open, impaled on the foot-long dildo that pokes up like a rude finger from the chair seat.

Kip opens his mouth. The groan that comes out is unmistakable, inevitable—the sound of a boy with a big one up his ass.

His nude flesh is glazed with sweat. It sparkles in the clefts of his broad, square shoulders, shimmers across the sleek expanse of his swimmer's pecs, trickles down the hard ridges of his belly. Beads of sweat hang suspended from his nipples. Sweat gathers at the tip of his nose, collects into a fat, glistening drop, and falls with a tiny splat directly onto the tip of his cock. The stubby little pole of flesh pokes up so stiff it quivers like a compass needle pointing north.

Kip sits alone in the room. Nude. Impaled. Erect. Waiting for the Big Shot.

The room is a grimy little one-room apartment, a fourth-floor walk-up in a tenement hotel on the bad side of town. The kind of hotel where people come and go and make a point of minding their own business. The kind of neighborhood where a gunshot or a scream hardly raises an eyebrow.

The room has a high ceiling with an old-fashioned ceiling fan, frozen with rust and covered with cobwebs. The dry, brittle wallpaper has faded to an anonymous gray, leaving no trace of its original color; in some places bare wooden slats show through. The threadbare carpet shows the ghost of an oriental pattern popular fifty years ago.

A few mattresses piled on the floor and a few chairs are the only furniture, except for a big trunk in one corner. The lid of the trunk is open. Odds and ends spill over the edges. Stained sheets and frayed towels. A length of rubber hose. A leather strap. A pair of sheer nylon pantihose with the crotch cut out. Police-issue handcuffs. The Big Shot's toy box.

Against one wall a commode sits unconcealed, in full view. The porcelain bowl is chipped and caked with grime. The seat lies discarded on the floor, split in two with its hinges broken. The paper dispenser is empty. The Big Shot doesn't use toilet paper. Instead, a strong, thin chain is padlocked around the cylinder with a clip at the end for a dog collar, like the one Kip wears around his neck—an arrangement the Big Shot calls a "French toilet."

Kip

Above the commode, an enema bag with a long plastic hose hangs from a hook on the wall.

The room is surrounded by mirrors, tall full-length mirrors in cheap wooden frames propped against the walls—mirrors everywhere, cracked and frosted with age, like mirrors in a junk store. Kip squirms behind his blindfold, unable to see his own reflection cast a thousand times around the squalid little room—a cute young blond just out of his teens, naked with a hard-on, sitting in a chair in the middle of the room, shivering and covered with sweat.

The day is a scorcher. The single narrow window is open, propped up by a toilet plunger jammed into the breach. The shadow of the plunger is cast in ripples against the thick, sun-bright drapes that shut out the breeze. *"Hot? You can open the window,"* Fagan told him, long ago when he dropped him off for his first meeting with the Big Shot. *"But you never open the drapes. Never. Understand me, pussyboy?"*

Kip understands. The broken-paned tenement across the street is empty and abandoned, but the Big Shot takes no chances on Peeping Toms. No witnesses. No grainy photos taken with telephoto lenses. What the Big Shot and his goon do to Kip in the grimy little room is a Big Secret.

Kip has been meeting the man for almost six months now. The visits follow no regular pattern. The very first time, the man rented him from Fagan for a whole week, keeping him locked and blindfolded in the hotel room day and night. The longest week of Kip's life—even Fagan coddled him afterwards, letting him rest at home with Uncle Max, knowing he was in no shape to work again for weeks afterward.

Usually the Big Shot wants him only for the night, sometimes for just a few hours. The man and his goon can do a lot to a boy like Kip in a few hours.

Sometimes it's twice a week, sometimes twice a month. Sometimes weeks pass without a word, and Kip can almost imagine the Big Shot has forgotten him—until the phone rings and Fagan tells him to have his ass on the curb in fifteen minutes. When the car starts heading for the freeway Kip knows what's coming. Like today. A few hours ago, Kip was just getting out of bed—a free day ahead, no regular johns on his calendar, Uncle Max busy at the hotel. Now he sits on the foot-long dildo, groaning and sweating, waiting for the Big Shot and his goon....

On the drive over, he asked Fagan if it was only for the night. Fagan laughed and wouldn't say.

It was already sweltering when they arrived. Fagan watched him open the window, smirking. *"Hot, baby? Maybe you should take off your clothes."* As if Kip had any choice.

Fagan leaned against the door, groping himself through his pants pocket, watching while Kip followed the ritual. Stripping off his sneakers and jeans, T-shirt and socks, and the crotch-pinching silk panties Uncle Max likes him to wear. Giving them to Fagan to take with him—the last he'll see of his clothes until Fagan returns. Reaching into the toy chest, putting on his dog collar. Oiling the crack of his ass. Walking to the chair—starting to tremble. Groaning when he saw the new dildo—a new one each time, each new one bigger than the last, like a pot plant shooting up between visits. The first had been hardly more than a buttplug. Today it was a genuine gut-wrencher—twelve inches straight up, beer-bottle thick at the crown, even thicker at the base.

It took him a long time to get settled on the thing. Grimacing, squatting, balancing himself like a monkey on the chair, trying to let himself down easy. Chewing his lips, squinting his eyes, letting out a

Kip

whimper and a hiss. Blushing hot all over at the sound of Fagan's laughter—and then the sound of Fagan's zipper going down.

Fagan helped him with the last few inches. A big, warm cock in his mouth made opening up for the dildo so much easier.

Watching always got Fagan hot. It didn't take him long to blow. Not in Kip's mouth. All over his face, for the Big Shot to see. Afterwards he let Kip lick him clean, squeezing out the last few drops on the boy's tongue. He wiped his cock on the blindfold, then tied the blindfold around Kip's head.

Blind, Kip descended into the world of sound and sensation. *"See ya later, cocksucker."* A hard slap across his face for no particular reason, making his ears ring. Fagan, laughing. Footsteps. The rattle of the doorknob. A creak and a slam—and Kip was alone....

Kip has been waiting for two hours now. He squirms in the chair. The taste of Fagan's semen lingers in his mouth, bitter and oily. His face still stings from the slap—nobody slaps harder than Karl Fagan. Not even the goon.

His buttocks ache against the hard, flat seat. The rubber horn up his ass is a constant torment. The pose is almost impossible to hold—sitting rigid and submissive in the chair at an angle just so, showing off the tender pink rim of his hole, shiny with oil and stretched paper thin around the base of the dildo. Just the way the man likes to see him when he walks through the door. Kip's muscles start to cramp, sweat pours down his body in sheets—but he doesn't dare to move. The Big Shot and his goon might arrive at any instant.

Two hours. The Big Shot has never been so late before. Perhaps he won't come at all—hope flutters in his chest, but Kip beats it down, knowing it's a lie. The man will show. Even if Kip has to sit and suffer on the dildo all day and night. Dazed by the heat, sick with dread, Kip almost wishes they'd hurry. Just to get it over with ...

Kip has never seen the Big Shot or his goon. *"The blindfold is for your protection,"* Fagan told him the first time. *"Don't get any stupid ideas about cheating. You let that thing 'accidentally' fall off while the man's porking your butt, and the next thing to come off are your balls. Not that anybody'd miss 'em."* Obviously the Big Shot is rich; most of Fagan's clients are. He must be famous as well; otherwise why keep Kip from ever seeing his face? And he travels—that would explain his random visits. Perhaps he doesn't even live in the city, and passes through only for the pleasure of spending a few stolen moments playing with his favorite toy.

The goon is his bodyguard; he calls the Big Shot "sir" and always carries a gun. Even naked, he wears it in a holster strapped across his chest. Kip has no trouble telling the two men apart.

The Big Shot is older, perhaps in his late forties. Salt-and-pepper hair—Kip knows from the black and silver pubic hairs he's plucked from his lips after a long afternoon of sucking the man's cock. He has a pleasant voice, velvety and deep. A con man's voice, but used to giving orders. Military man, movie star, politician, preacher?

The Big Shot is a big man, unusually tall—kneeling beneath him, Kip has to strain his neck to take the man's balls in his mouth, or to push his tongue up the man's asshole. He has a firm, athletic body, with powerful arms—strong enough to hold Kip down. Strong enough to knock him halfway across the room when Kip moves too slow.

Kip

The goon is much younger. Kip imagines him in his early twenties, fresh out of college, a bodyguard with a bachelor's degree. He has an terse, educated way of talking, as if every word were a shiny piece of silver—until he starts talking dirty. He has a hard, pumped-up physique—hairy legs knotted with muscle, a sleek, sculpted chest and belly, biceps and shoulders like stacked-up grapefruits. A carrot-top—the crotch hair he leaves in Kip's mouth is like shiny copper wire, sharp and abrasive against the tender lips of Kip's mouth and ass.

The goon has a mean cock.

The Big Shot's dick is larger, almost a match for Fagan's—a huge, veiny slab of flesh covered with a drooping mass of foreskin, with a piss-slit so large Kip can stick his tongue in halfway to the root. But, even at its hardest, the Big Shot's pole has a rubbery, spongy texture, like a layer of fat wrapped around gristle, a plump, padded cock, sliding up Kip's ass or stuffing his throat with a certain ease.

There's nothing soft or gentle about the goon's cock—a cock like a weapon, like a missile. Thinking about it takes Kip's breath away—constantly erect and dribbling and stiff as a broom handle, even after he's come, attached to a pair of hips like a steam-driven piston. A cock that could drive rivets into steel. Relentless. Devastating. Brutal. A cruel cock, a cock with no mercy. He can fuck for hours.

Kip goes dizzy behind his blindfold, remembering, dreading it—then he stiffens. A sound from the hallway outside …

Footsteps. But not the Big Shot, because the Big Shot never comes without his goon, and Kip hears only a single set of steps: right, left, right, left. Not from the stairwell, but from farther down the hall. Perhaps it's Fagan, returning. Kip's heart beats faster at the thought. He imagines the door swinging open and Fagan laughing, his lips drawn back in a thin, condescending smile. *Show's over, cocksucker. Just a little joke—blind man's buff. The man's not coming after all. Had you fooled, didn't I?*

The footsteps slow, and come to a complete halt just beyond the locked door. Kip's heart booms inside his chest. He imagines he can hear a hand on the doorknob—then the footsteps turn and walk away, back in the direction they came from. Just a stranger in the hall, probably drunk and confused ...

And suddenly Kip realizes that he's never heard anyone in the hallway before, except for Fagan, and the Big Shot and his goon. And though the walls must be paper thin, he's never heard a sound from either of the adjacent rooms. In fact, he's never seen or heard a soul up here on the fourth floor, as if the Big Shot had the whole story reserved for himself. Yet, as Kip listens, the footsteps shuffle quietly back down the hallway, until a door creaks open and clicks shut.

Someone is in the next room.

Kip listens intently, his hearing heightened behind the blindfold. But the only sounds are the beating of his own heart and the listless rustling of the drapes. Then he forgets about the footsteps—about everything else—as he bends forward in pain.

The cramp begins suddenly, high up in his bowels—a ring of muscle abruptly clamping tight around the very head of the thick rubber shaft deep in his guts. Kip shivers and groans. The spasm works its way downward, like a ring of lips undulating down the dildo. Kip pouts. Kip moans, flexing his bowels to resist the inevitable. Finally he lets out a long, sputtering fart. The lips of his ass smack wetly against the rubber base with a snap, crackle, pop. Alone in the room, Kip blushes bright red around his nipples and ears. He groans and hangs his head in shame. His cock is hard as a rock.

And at that moment the door swings open.

"Well, look who's here, sitting pretty."

"Pretty as a picture, sir."

"And with egg on his face."

"I think it's dried come, sir."

The door slams. The voices circle around him.

"And he looks excited to see us. If he could see. Well, Kippy. What's up?"

A snigger: "What's up his *ass*, you mean."

Kip grimaces with the effort to hold it back. Useless. He cuts another fart, louder and wetter than the first. The men laugh so hard they cackle. Kip's nipples harden and his skin turns to gooseflesh. The Big Shot and his goon have arrived....

In the room next door, amid the rubble of cast-off furniture and broken lamps, Uncle Max crouches quiet as a church mouse beside the wall. His heart pounds in his chest, he struggles to keep from wheezing. They almost caught him. If he hadn't heard them coming up the stairs ... He was crazy to venture into the hallway in the first place. But after two hours of crouching by the peephole, watching Kip sitting and suffering in the chair, he could hardly stand it anymore.

And if he'd gone through with it? What a scene that would have made. Max bursting into the room, pulling off Kip's blindfold. *"Enough of this, Kip! I'm taking you home, son, where you belong."* Helping the boy up from the chair, easing him off the big dildo with a *pop*, throwing a seedy blanket over his shoulders. A daring rescue—Kip's warm, naked body all smooth and supple beneath the blanket, shivering in his uncle's protective embrace, his perpetual little hard-on poking against Max's thigh. *"Oh, Uncle Max—oh, my hero!"*

And then, of course, they'd have run into the two creeps in the hallway—and that would have been the end of it. The redhead carries a gun. Max can see the bulge of the shoulder holster inside his jacket.

Besides, Max didn't come here to rescue Kip.

Max came to take pictures.

Because Max knows who the Big Shot is.

For months, after Fagan first got his clutches into them, Max spent every waking moment trying to figure a way out of the vice-cop's box. Finally he quit banging his head against the wall. Fagan has them jammed into a corner too tight. No way out.

Even so, it galls him—every time Fagan and his boys drop by in the middle of the night, yanking Kip out of bed, taking turns slapping him around and banging his ass and making Max watch and serve drinks from the bar. Every time Kip disappears for a few hours on a quiet Sunday afternoon and comes back with swollen nipples and strap marks on his ass. Every time Max comes home and a john is still there, and he can hear the squeals from Kip's bedroom. Fagan seems to specialize in a clientele of rich old toads who like to play rough with a boy like Kip. Sometimes Max can hardly stand it.

Max has given up hope of escape. Karl Fagan is the most powerful pimp in the city. Karl Fagan is also the city's number-one vice cop. Fagan has all the bases covered. Everybody owes him. Nobody dares to cross him.

But as long as things have to stay as they are, why shouldn't Max get his own cut of the profits from Kip's sweet young ass? After all, Kip is his, in a way. He's the one who brought Kip to the city, gave him

Kip

honest work at the hotel, invited him to share his own plush apartment. All he asked in return was an occasional ride on his darling nephew's back and an occasional blow inside his warm, wet mouth. It's not Max's fault if Kip started peddling his ass to strangers and caught Fagan's attention. Kip brought it all on himself and dragged Max along with him.

So why shouldn't Max get something out of it, besides an occasional black eye from Fagan and his creeps? Something substantial, the kind of nest egg he could comfortably retire on—the kind of filthy lucre that comes only from robbing a bank, or selling crack to school kids, or peddling missiles to crazy Arabs.

Or blackmail.

Max has been hearing about the Big Shot from the beginning. Sometimes, late at night, Kip still creeps into Max's bedroom and snuggles up next to him, looking for a friendly ear to listen. The Big Shot is the worst of them all, cruel and abusive with a singularly filthy imagination. Listening in the dark to all the atrocious things he's done to Kip always brings out the soft spot in Max's heart—and the hard-on between his legs. *There, there, it'll be all right,* he coos, guiding Kip's mouth down to his raging erection. *Tell me again—I can't believe he'd do that to you,* he gasps, slipping his cock into the tight, moist recess of Kip's asshole.

Each time Fagan has taken him to service the Big Shot, Kip has spilled his guts to Max afterwards. Slowly a pattern emerged—call it intuition, luck, circumstance. Max read the papers, watched the news, and suddenly noticed a correlation between Kip's meetings and visits to the city by a certain very powerful, very high-profile public official. A tall, handsome politician with salt-and-pepper hair, always accompanied by a coterie of publicity people and attendants—one of them a surly-faced young bodyguard with curly red hair.

Step one was finding out from Kip the location of the seedy hotel room.

Step two was arranging to rent a room next door. The manager, a shifty-eyed Rastafarian who reeked of ganja, was hesitant, even in the face of several Ben Franklins.

It seemed that one individual reserved the entire space of the fourth floor. Max persevered. Max emptied his wallet. Ah, well, since it seemed that the gentleman who rented the fourth floor was seldom in town and never used any but a single room, perhaps (with a bloodshot wink and a smirk) the manager could allow Max access to a small room. Hardly more than a closet, really; he would have to put up with all the odds and ends stored there....

Step three was buying the camera and drilling the hole.

Step four was patience. He didn't have long to wait. Three days ago, Max read in a society column that a certain bigwig was in town, addressing an international trade conference. The next day he overheard Fagan and one of his creeps, zipping up their trousers outside Kip's bedroom after a lunch-hour quickie.

"What a fucking mouth, huh, boss? Thanks for the freebie."

"Sure thing. And listen, don't schedule any johns for the kid for the rest of the week."

"Oh, yeah? You gonna give his ass a thousand-mile checkup or something?"

"Wise guy. Nah, the kid's gonna be busy. Taking him for another session with—let's just say a very important client. Starting Wednesday afternoon."

Kip

Bingo!

Max presses his face to the wall and squints through the hole. The view is like a framed picture—Kip in the center, nude and glistening in the soft yellow light, the redhead behind him, the Big Shot in front. The man stands at an angle, his back to the peephole; Max still can't see his face, just the long, trim cut of his black silk suit and the glossy shine of his patent-leather shoes. The redhead's jacket is already off, along with his shirt. His hands are busy strapping the shoulder holster across his superbly muscled chest.

The two men exchange words—Max can't quite hear. Suddenly the redhead smirks, raises one foot to the back of the chair, and gives it a hard shove. Kip squeals and falls forward, banging his knees against the floor, landing on his outstretched hands. The dildo stays buried in his ass, bringing the chair with it.

The men exchange glances. The redhead flashes a grin like a twelve-year-old, then glances back to Kip. The dildo is starting to ooze from his ass. The redhead uses his foot against the bottom of the chair to grind it back in. Kip's face is pressed against the filthy carpet, contorted with suffering. He seems to be staring through his blindfold, straight at the peephole. The illusion is so disturbing that Max flinches and draws back by reflex.

His heart thumps inside his flabby chest. His cock is stiff and bent inside his trousers. He struggles not to squeeze it. He's already come in his pants twice—once while watching Kip squirm on the dildo, and earlier, watching him blow Fagan. He thought for sure they'd heard him that time, huffing and puffing as he shot. With the redhead and his pistol, he doesn't dare take any chances. Quiet as a church mouse ...

"Up on your hands and feet, cunt." The redhead's

voice carries through the wall. Max bends down to the peephole again.

Kip is up on all fours, his knees and elbows braced, cantering about the room like a drunken pony. The redhead follows behind, laughing, holding the chair by two legs and using the dildo to prod Kip along. No matter how fast Kip canters the dildo stays in his ass, plowing in and out, in and out, jabbing to the left and right, making him squeal when it pokes especially hard against his prostate. Loosened by the prolonged penetration, his ass squelches and farts around the rubber shaft. His balls slap up against the underside of his cock. His cock slaps against his belly and dribbles on the carpet. Max squints and chews his lower lip.

For an instant, the redhead and Kip pass out of the frame. Max's attention is drawn back to the Big Shot. The man stands with his head thrown back in amusement, loosening his tie. Slipping off his jacket, draping it over the back of a hideous overstuffed purple chair. He makes a three-quarter turn, keeping his eye on Kip and the bodyguard. Finally Max has the chance to see his face....

Except that Max is momentarily distracted by the thing hanging from the open fly of the Big Shot's baggy dress slacks.

Ugly, Max thinks to himself, feeling a powerful twinge of pure male envy. *Big and ugly.*

The Big Shot doesn't have a pretty cock. The Big Shot doesn't need one. Nine inches of solid meat hang out of his pants fly, sheathed in a wrinkled mass of foreskin corrugated with pencil-thick veins. Beneath the hood of skin, the very tip of his plump cockhead is visible, glinting wetly and dribbling a long, suspended thread of milky fluid. Max can smell it through the peephole.

Kip

An ugly cock. No doubt about it. Max has never seen an uglier one. His mouth begins to water.

After all, though it's been a long while, once upon a time Max was a hungry young cocksucker himself. It's been years since he really went down on a man. True, occasionally he teases Kip with a playful suck, but that hardly counts. Kip has a cocktail weenie between his legs; the Big Shot has a double-thick salami. It's been a long, long time since Max had a cock in his mouth like the Big Shot's. From ancient instinct, his jaw goes slack. His stomach growls.

Even as he stares, the long, drooping slab of meat begins to stir and thicken, twitching in the hot, musty air. The Big Shot reaches into his fly and pulls out his balls. The sack of flesh fills the cup of his hand and spills over the edges. He gives them a squeeze, then lets them tumble free—as big and ugly as his cock, hanging full and loose in a wrinkled sack of translucent flesh.

Max licks his lips and swallows. So distracted he almost forgets what he came for. Finally he tears his eyes from the man's cock and takes a look at his face.

Bingo.

It's him. No doubt about it. Unsurprised, Max nevertheless lets out a stifled gasp, astonished at the enormity of it. Suddenly Fagan seems like small potatoes.

Max knows a lot about the Big Shot. Max has been reading up in *People* and *Newsweek*.

Ex-Ivy League football quarterback. Ex-marine colonel with two tours of duty in Vietnam. Family man and dedicated Southern Baptist with two sons in college and a debutante daughter. Right-wing Republican senior senator from a prominent Sunbelt state. Jogs ten miles every day come rain or shine and teaches ghetto boys boxing down at the Y. All-around Big Shot.

The news rags never mention that he has a dick that hangs nine inches soft. Or that he likes to use it on bent-over blond ass. Or that he gets his kicks by putting the screws to a piece of male pussy in a dog collar in a dingy little hotel room on the wrong side of the tracks. The Big Shot has a Big Secret. Until now only the goon and Karl Fagan shared it. Now Uncle Max knows it, too. His fingers tremble as he reaches for the camera.

The light in the room is perfect. The focus is automatic. The shutter and film advance are utterly silent. Thank God for German engineering.

Max presses the button—and captures the Big Shot with his hands on his hips, his cock jutting semi-stiff from his fly, a smirk on his face. Very different from the image on his campaign posters.

"Bring the faggot over here, Smitty."

The redhead has a name. Probably made up for Kip's benefit. As phony as the Big Shot's campaign promises.

Kips stamps around the room in an awkward circuit, banging his elbows against chairs, bouncing across mattresses. The redhead follows at a casual pace, using the chair like a steering wheel. He guides Kip back to the center of the room and parks him ass up on all fours at the Big Shot's feet.

Kip pants like a sprinter after a race. Sweat pours from his bent-over body like rain from a tent. The chair heaves atop his rearing buttocks like a howdah on an elephant's back. The redhead pulls up on the chair legs, almost pulling the fat, shiny dildo free of Kip's sphincter—then stabs it all the way in again.

"Kiss my feet, faggot."

Kip blubbers. Why does the goon have to be so

cruel? He follows his nose to the Big Shot's feet, sniffing saddle soap and shoe polish. He presses his lips against the hard, shiny leather.

"Better than that." The Big Shot wriggles his foot and gives a little kick, grinning down at the sight of Kip's face stretched like a blowfish around the widest part of his shoe.

"Let the faggot sit down again, Smitty."

The redhead grabs the chair back with one hand and a fistful of Kip's hair with the other, pulling upward and back. The chair crashes upright on the floor. Kip slides down the pole, like a cardboard clown on a stick. His sweaty buttocks slap the wood. Kip squeals. His cock quivers and squirts. The Big Shot slaps his face.

"What's the matter, fagboy? Your pussy getting too much of a good thing?"

If only Max had thought to bring a tape recorder as well ...

"Up on your feet, faggot."

Kip struggles to stand and makes a complete fool of himself. His arms and legs are rubbery from scrambling. The dildo pokes into him too deeply. He flails like a spastic, unable to achieve lift off. Helpless. Trapped. The redhead smacks him across the back of the head. The Big Shot snorts in disgust. "Can't even stand up like a man."

He grabs a fistful of Kip's hair and pulls him to his feet with a single jerk. The liquid *plop* is even louder than Kip's squeal. The naked boy wobbles like a marionette, held up by the fist in his hair.

The Big Shot draws him close, looking him up and down.

Kip has a beautiful body. Even after all the abuse of the past few months—if anything, more beautiful now that when the Big Shot first met him. Fagan makes sure that he sticks to his regimen of swimming and lifting weights. His muscles are long and lean, perfectly proportioned, just beginning to show a bodybuilder's pump. His shoulders are broad and square, his pectorals big and superbly shaped, his nipples plump and glossy. A firm, rippling belly and hard lean hips. A perfect all-over tan—Kip sunbathes nude on the deck of Uncle Max's apartment. His skin is the color of honey, smoother than silk, soft as a baby's bottom all over. Completely hairless except for the tiny patch of blond between his legs ...

The Big Shot's dick jerks and reaches maximum erection. It pokes like a clenched fist against Kip's midriff. His voice is unexpectedly soft in Kip's ear. "Such a pretty, pretty boy. Are you glad to see me, Kip?"

Kip shudders. Confused. Shaken. "Yes, sir."

"Liar." The Big Shot chuckles softly. "You should never lie to me, Kip." He gently strokes the boy's cheek, smooth and downy against the back of his hand. Then he draws back and punches Kip in the belly, holding him upright by the hair, watching in fascination as the muscles of Kip's torso clench and spasm. He punches again.

"Sir?"

"Yes? What is it, Smitty?"

"Sir, I thought you'd want to know. There's shit on this dildo."

"Shit?"

"Yes, sir. From the faggot's ass, sir."

"Well. We'll have to do something about that." He draws back and gives Kip a final punch, letting go of his hair at the same time. Kip bends double from the pain. The man shoves him to his hands and knees, then kicks him hard to set him crawling in the right direction.

Kip

"Get your ass to the toilet, faggot."

Max swings the camera at an angle and cranes his neck to see through the viewfinder. He presses the button just as Kip enters the frame, crawling on his hands and knees. The Big Shot walks beside him, smirking, pulling on the huge, blood-gorged pole of flesh jutting from his fly. The redhead waits beside the toilet, grinning like a demented twelve-year-old. In one hand he holds the twelve-inch dildo, detached from the chair seat. In the other he holds the yellow enema bag....

Kip stands with his legs planted far apart, bent over in front of the commode. His face is in the bowl. His hands are on his cheeks, pulling them wide open. His exposed hole glistens with lubricant and tiny beads of water.

The Big Shot stands beside him, holding the twelve-inch dildo and slapping it against the palm of his hand. The rubber is clean as a whistle now, shiny with Kip's saliva. Kip dirtied it with one hole. Kip cleaned it with the other. With each smack against his open palm, the man's own cock gives a little jerk, poking stiff and fleshy from his open fly.

He looks down at Kip, sweaty and shivering, naked except for his blindfold and dog collar. He curls his upper lip. "Give him another one, Smitty."

The redhead smiles. "Yes, sir. With pleasure, sir." He submerges the yellow enema bag in the open toilet tank.

"No, please, not any more ..." Kip's sobbing sounds hollow and strange, echoing up from the toilet bowl.

"Shut your dirty mouth, fagboy. For that you'll take two more bags." The Big Shot raises his foot and plants it on Kip's head, pushing his face into the bowl. While Kip gurgles and spews, the redhead pulls the bloated enema bag from the tank and holds it aloft with one hand, spearing the nozzle into Kip's rectum with the other.

The bag rapidly wilts, emptying another half-gallon into Kip's bowels.

The Big Shot relents and pulls his foot away. Kip emerges from the bowl coughing and sputtering. The wet blindfold clings to his face. His golden hair is matted against his forehead, sopping wet. "No, please, I can't stand it, please stop!"

The Big Shot tosses the dildo to the floor. He squeezes his cock, fondling the great drooping mass of veiny foreskin that sheathes the core. "Three more bags, Smitty."

"Yes, sir …"

In the next room, Uncle Max pulls his camera from the peephole. He leans against the wall and mops his face with a handkerchief. The day keeps getting hotter and hotter—it would help if he could take off some clothes, but the movement might make too much noise. Not that the Big Shot or his goon would be likely to hear anything with the toilet tank running and Kip begging them to stop. The ordeal has been going on now for more than an hour. Kip keeps emptying his guts in the toilet. The redhead keeps filling him up again.

Max takes a break from shooting. How many pictures of the redhead giving Kip an enema can he use, anyway? Over and over. The Big Shot won't relent. Kip's pleading only seems to egg him on. Surely at some point they'll have to stop. Max mops his forehead and shuts his eyes—

Then opens them again, realizing the running water has stopped. He must have dozed off, just for a minute. He turns his head and peers through the hole….

Kip

The Big Shot is relaxing in the huge, overstuffed purple chair beside the window, stripped below the waist to boxer shorts and black socks. His dress shirt is open, his tie unknotted. In one hand he holds a jumbo-size can of cold beer. In the other he holds his erect cock, jutting up from the fly of his trunks, kneading and squeezing it, rubbing his palm over the exposed crown. Max would be hard-pressed to say which is thicker; the can or the cock. As for length, there's no contest. The Big Shot is hung.

Again Max feels a powerful flash of jealousy mixed with desire, and not just because of the man's cock. He and the Big Shot are practically the same age; Max might even be younger. But some men age better than others.

The Big Shot has all the right genes. The Big Shot had all the right breaks. Ivy League football, marines, lifelong physical fitness enthusiast. *"As young as you feel"* ran the caption in *People* magazine, showing the senator out for his morning jog. *"A man's man"* said *Time,* beneath a photo of the Big Shot in boxing trunks holding his own against a kid half his age at an exhibition match for charity. The kind of pictures secretaries tack to the wall and moon over at coffee break. The kind of body a man Max's age would kill to have. Thick, sturdy legs. A hard, ridged belly. Shoulders and arms that look impressive even in a suit. A deep, broad chest. The muscular cleavage exposed between the starched panels of his shirt is densely matted with hair, all salt and pepper, like the hair on his head.

While the Big Shot takes a break, Kip waits beside the chair. The bright, diffused light from the drapes shimmers across his sweaty flesh, sculpting highlights and casting deep shadows, making his nude body gleam as if it were carved from wax. He stands with his head bowed and his arms behind him, reaching back to hold his buttocks together. His stubby little cock stands rigid at attention. His chest heaves up and down. A clothespin is attached to each throbbing nipple. *Tenderizing his tits,* the Big Shot calls it, getting them sensitive and swollen to play with later.

Kip's shoulders heave as if he were sobbing; he trembles as if he were chilled with fever. He opens his mouth to speak, then stops himself at the last instant, biting his lower lip. His eyebrows draw together. Finally he opens his mouth again. His voice breaks and the best he can manage is a blubbering whine. "Please—oohhhh, please, sir, please let me …"

The Big Shot takes a swig of beer. Squeezes his cock. Looks Kip up and down and purses his lips. The very picture of a man with a hard-on in the heat of the day, just starting to feel a buzz …

With a flick of his wrist he presses the frosty can against the underbelly of Kip's hard-on, pulling a deep, plaintive moan from the boy. The moan rises in pitch when he presses the can between Kip's legs, chilling his little ball-sack and the tender inner flesh of his thighs.

Kip squeezes his eyes shut and shakes his head. His shoulders give a convulsive jerk. "Please …"

"Quit your whining, faggot."

"Please, I need to let it out, real bad … The cramps—"

"Not yet. Hold your cheeks together, boy, tight. That's the only way, Kip. You make another mess, the way you did last time, and I'll have to punish you again. You remember last time, how I punished you?"

Kip's chest heaves, suddenly short of breath. He flushes bright red. "Yes, sir."

"You wouldn't want that to happen again, would you?"

Kip

"No, please, no, sir."

"Then don't fuck up, Kip. Stop whining. Act like a man." The Big Shot brings the beer to his lips and turns it upright, downing the rest of the can. He tosses it aside, wipes his mouth with the back of his hand—then abruptly lashes out and punches Kip in the belly. Oceans churn and slosh as he bends double from the pain, but Kip keeps his cheeks pressed together and his sphincter clamped tight.

Behind him the redhead snorts with laughter. "Four to one the faggot can't hold it, sir."

"I never gamble, Smitty. A weak man's vice. Stand up straight, fagboy." The Big Shot sits forward in his chair. He reaches up and flicks his middle finger against the clothespins that hang from Kip's nipples, watching them bob up and down, listening to Kip hiss. He trails his fingers down the sweat-slick undulations of Kip's belly, counting the ridges above his navel, spreading his fingers across the flat, hairless expanse of his groin. He plays with Kip's hard-on, slapping it back and forth, tugging at the hair on his balls, pinching the very tip of the boy's penis between his fingernail and thumb.

"He has a pretty little cock, don't you think, Smitty?"

"I never really noticed, sir. I suppose so, for a faggot. If you think it's big enough to call it a cock."

Kip blushes and groans. His nipples ache. His cock is hot and throbbing. He has to press hard to keep his cheeks together. Kip has never needed to take a dump so badly in his life.

The Big Shot keeps teasing him with one hand, fondling himself with the other. He caresses Kip's thigh, feeling the gooseflesh rise beneath his fingertips. "Beautiful skin. All sleek and hairless. Smooth as silk. A shame about this hairy patch between his legs." He strokes the sleek blond nest at the base of Kip's cock, pinches a half-dozen strands between his finger and thumb and and plucks them out by the roots. Kip opens his mouth in a silent gasp.

"Look in my briefcase, Smitty. Bring me another beer. And while you're at it, get out the shaving soap and that straight razor...."

Max can't help it. For the third time today, Max is about to come in his pants.

Watching them shave Kip's crotch has him hotter than he's felt in months. It's been a fantasy of Max's for a long time, ever since Kip first moved in with him. First he was too bashful to suggest it—Kip would see him for the letch he was. Then Fagan entered the picture, and Max was afraid the vice cop wouldn't like it—Kip is a commodity, and not every john wants a pussyboy with a bald crotch.

Kip stands over the toilet. The Big Shot stands behind him, kissing and nibbling his neck, whispering obscenities in his ear, tugging the clothespins from his chest and snapping them back onto his aching nipples.

Kip seems to be in agony—quivering, whining, spasming in strange little jerks. His shoulders, arms and chest strain and flex from the effort of keeping his buttocks pressed together. Max can see the steady trickle of water running down the insides of his legs.

Meanwhile the redhead sits on a stool beside the commode, using old-fashioned shaving soap and a brush to moisten Kip's crotch, then scraping him smooth with a shiny straight razor brand-new from the box. Denuding his crotch with a few careful strokes. Shaving away the curls at the base of his hard-on. Making him spread his legs to let his little balls hang free while the redhead scrapes the blade up and down the tender flesh.

Kip

Max snaps a final photo, holding the camera with one hand, squeezing his crotch furiously with the other. Kip is such a jewel, more beautiful every day. If only Max could still call him his own, his darling boy....

The redhead towels the last of the cream from between Kip's legs and leans back, wiping his hands. Kip is revealed. Humiliated. Denuded. Naked and erect. Max stifles a groan and fills his underwear with jism.

For a brief moment, the orgasm strikes him deaf and blind, saving him from having to witness the spectacle that ensues, as Kip, desperate beyond any sense of shame, squats bowlegged over the toilet and empties his bowels noisily into the commode, to a chorus of laughter from the Big Shot and his goon....

Afternoon approaches evening. The light in the room begins to soften. Soon Max's camera will be useless—and the things he most needs to photograph are just beginning to happen....

All three are naked now. The muscular young redhead is stripped down to his shoulder holster, the Big Shot to his black socks and garters. Both men wear wedding bands, gold and glittery in the fading light.

All three naked. All three erect. Glistening with sweat in the stuffy little room. Naked flesh seems to paper the walls, reflected in fragments in the mirrors all around.

Kip stands before the Big Shot, arms at his sides. Eyes closed. Fingers clenching and unclenching. Sick from the suspense of awaiting his next humiliation. The man runs his fingertips over Kip's sleek chest and belly, down to the denuded flesh between his legs. Kips flinches at the touch, strangely cool and clammy.

"Sensitive, Kip? Happens sometimes, when a boy gets his first shave. Smitty—look in my briefcase again. See if there's not some kind of ointment in there. Something cool and soothing."

Kip waits silently behind his blindfold, then lets out a gasp when the man pulls the clothespins from his chest with a snap. His nipples tingle and throb, like a sleeping limb coming back to life. He gasps again when the man begins to pinch and squeeze the aching nubs between his fingers, rubbing something slick and creamy into the swollen flesh.

"There, Kip. Feel better?"

"I—I guess so."

"Here. I'll put some between your legs." The Big Shot fondles the boy's hairless balls with one hand, stroking and pulling on his little hard-on with the other. The pleasure is so sudden and so intense that Kip goes weak in the knees. The man's hand feels so good. Kip needs release so badly.

Then his nipples begin to burn.

The Big Shot pauses for a moment to squeeze more ointment from the tube, then spreads it all over Kip's denuded scrotum and cock, between his legs and behind his balls, stuffing it into his piss slit. The liniment is icy blue in color, and feels oddly cool when it first hits the skin. But the label tells another story, in red and orange letters shaped like little flames: *"HOT-AS-HELL Deep Heating Gel, for Relief of Stiff, Achy Muscles—Ten Times Hotter Than the Leading Ointment! Long-Lasting, Too!"*

The longer the Big Shot rubs, the deeper the ointment penetrates, and the hotter it gets. Kip's nipples are abruptly on fire, as if someone had touched them with a glowing match. Then the heat begins to flare between his legs.

"Oh, no. Oh, please, don't—"

Kip

"What's the matter, Kip? Don't you like having your little weenie roasted?"

"Oh, no, please, let me wash it off!"

"You didn't answer me, fagboy. Doesn't it feel good, getting your cock jerked off?"

"Yes—No—"

The Big Shot shrugs. He gives Kip's cock a stinging open-handed slap. The little pole of flesh sputters like a flaming torch.

"What kind of boy is it, doesn't like having his cock played with? Guess you're the type who'd rather take it up his ass." The Big Shot spins him around and bends him over. "Grab your ankles, faggot."

Grinning, waiting for the moment, already wearing his own and lubed up for the occasion, the redhead hands him a baggy sheepskin rubber. The Big Shot positions it at the crown of his cock and carefully rolls it down to the base. He squirts a handful of the liniment into his palm and strokes it up and down the condom, icing it with a thick coating of blue gel. Then he pushes the half-empty tube into the crack of Kip's ass, inserts the nozzle as far as it can reach into the boy's hole, and squeezes hard. A second later, he tosses the empty tube to the floor. Kip is already starting to quake and whimper in a strange, strangled voice.

The Big Shot gives his sheathed cock a final squeeze. Bone-hard and ready for total penetration. "Ever fucked a bucking bronco, Smitty?"

"No, sir. Can't say that I have."

"Watch and learn. You're up next...."

Afternoon fades into evening. Lit by a single lamp on the floor in one corner, the room becomes an uncertain, deep-shadowed place, endlessly reflected by the mirrors all around. Beyond the peephole, Max's camera lies discarded beside him, useless in the dark. No matter—he has all the pictures he needs, and then some. Still, he squats next to the wall, his eye pressed to the opening, unable to stop watching.

Max is exhausted. He came in his pants again, watching them bang Kip's ass. First the Big Shot, then the redhead. Then both came back for seconds. Fucking Kip every which way around the room. Bent over, grabbing his ankles. Down on his knees doggie-style. Doing his drunken-pony walk on his hands and feet.

When they both fucked him together, Max shot his fourth wad of the day. The Big Shot settled back in his easy chair with Kip on his lap, impaled on his big cock. Then he grabbed the boy's ankles and held his legs up in the air like a wishbone. The redhead moved in for the kill, hard as steel, sliding his cock up Kip's quim with a single stroke. The Big Shot had to hold Kip in place with his strong right arm while he covered his mouth with the other—even in this squalid hotel, a scream like that might attract attention.

The Big Shot and the redhead came at the same time, pressed dick to dick inside Kip's ass. An instant later, Max unloaded in his pants.

Now the room is quiet, for the moment at least. The redhead sits on a rumpled mattress, leaning back against the wall, smoking a cigarette. Looking sexy in his leather shoulder holster and nothing else. His cock pokes up stiff as a pipe against his washboard belly, as if he'd never come. But then, Max's cock is hard again, too, already stiff and throbbing in his come-filled trousers. Something about being around Kip does that to a man....

The Big Shot relaxes in the big purple chair, suck-

Kip

ing on a beer while Kip crouches between his legs and sucks on the man's big, satisfied cock, catching the dribblings that spurt out from time to time. He finishes the beer and tosses it aside, then shoves Kip's face from his crotch.

As soon as his mouth is empty, Kip starts to beg. "Please—"

"Shut your hole, cuntface. What a whiner." The Big Shot reaches down and retrieves his black silk tie from the floor. He wraps one end around the base of his cock and balls, making the big tube plump up like a bloated sausage. "First you kept begging to dump the enema. Now you're begging me to give you another one."

"Please, it still burns...."

"Red-hot pussy," Smitty croons, taking a drag off his cigarette.

"It burns—"

The Big Shot shuts him up by plugging a fistful of cock down his throat. He loops the tie twice around Kip's neck and ties a knot, binding him to his crotch, wearing the boy's face like a codpiece. The big man leans back in the chair with a look of ecstatic relief on his face. Kip's eyes are shut tight, his throat undulating as he swallows over and over.

"Smitty." The Big Shot's voice is languid and dreamy.

"Yes, sir."

"Put on some pants and a jacket. Run down to that little mom-and-pop store on the corner. Buy us another six-pack. And see if they've got another tube of that hot stuff. I'm getting in the mood to fuck somebody again."

"Yes, sir." The redhead slips into his socks and pulls on his pants sitting down. "And may I say thanks again for inviting me along, sir. Especially since we have the whole week to look forward to. I can't think of a more enjoyable or relaxing way to spend my vacation, sir."

Kip groans around the cock in his mouth. A week—seven days and seven nights of hell, locked blindfolded in the squalid little room, having his holes fucked raw while the man and his goon outdo each other thinking up new ways to torment him ...

"Think nothing of it, Smitty. You're a damn good kid. Damn good bodyguard." The Big Shot burps drunkenly.

Which sounds nothing at all like the noise that echoes from somewhere beyond the wall to his left.

Because, at that instant, in the first still, quiet hour after sunset, Max suddenly releases an uncontrollable and very noisy fart.

The Big Shot bolts forward in his chair, causing Kip to choke and gag. His voice is quiet, controlled, completely sober. "Smitty ..."

But the redhead doesn't need to be told. He springs from the mattress like a cat, his gun already drawn, opens the door and bolts into the hallway.

A loud banging. A crash. Splintering wood. Objects knocked aside and a muffled gasp. Five seconds later Smitty steps through the doorway again, dragging Max by one ear, holding the pistol to his head. Both of them are breathing hard.

"Next room over, sir. Crouching by a peephole—there, you can see it, between those slats. With a fucking camera, sir!" He unslings it from his shoulder and throws it to the floor.

The Big Shot stands, bringing Kip with him. Kip flails and gags, tied to the man's crotch, strangling on his cock.

"Alone, Smitty?"

"As far as I could tell, sir."

Kip

"Anything besides the camera—tape recorder, videocam?" The Big Shot's voice is steady, no-nonsense, in charge. But his heart is beating like a jackrabbit's. Kip can tell from the pulse throbbing through the cock in his throat.

"Not that I could see, sir—just the camera."

"Fucking amateur. Handcuff the sonofabitch to the toilet pipe, Smitty. Then check the other rooms up the hall. Then go down to the front desk and get Fagan on the phone. Tell that crooked pimp I want his ass over here in five minutes flat."

"Right, sir." The redhead shoves Max against the wall, reaches into the toy box, handcuffs him to the fuzzy black pipe. "You don't really think Fagan was in on this, do you, sir?"

"How the hell else would fatso here know—unless ..." As the redhead hurries down the hall, the Big Shot looks down at the blindfolded face attached to his cock. He looks up at Max. "Who the fuck are you, anyway?"

"I—look, mister, I didn't mean anything by taking the pictures, I just wanted 'em for my own use, you know—"

At the sound of Max's voice, Kip's eyebrows shoot above the blindfold. He squeals around the big, throbbing cock, making it hum like a tuning fork. Three syllables, indecipherable except as a strangling gurgle: *Uncle Max!*

As if he could hear the words through his dick, the Big Shot stares at Max with sudden comprehension. "You're the kid's uncle, aren't you? The prissy old queen he lives with. Yeah, Fagan told me all about you—you're the one who started selling the boy's ass in the first place, right? Till Fagan nudged you out. Jesus, so you're the dirty old fart who copped the kid's cherry, huh? Crawled into your nephew's bunk one night and turned him into your private little sperm bank."

"Please, mister," Max blubbers. "Please, I don't wanna make any trouble, honest—"

"So who else is in on this, fatso? Huh? The kid, for sure?"

"No! No, Kip doesn't know anything about it, honest! You have to believe me!"

Uncle Max! Kip gurgles again, and then, in a panic, he reaches up to undo his blindfold.

"No! Kip, stop! Stop him, he doesn't know anything, I beg you!..."

Kip pushes the blindfold up to his forehead. For an instant he sees the Big Shot's hard, flat belly, matted with salt-and-pepper swirls, so close to his nose he can't focus. He turns his head as far as he can, just enough to catch a glimpse of Max chained to the pipe, shaking his head and crying like a baby.

The redhead rushes in. Kip had no idea he was so good looking. Even more muscular than he'd thought, incredibly sexy in his tight slacks and leather holster. Big arms. Sleek chest. Washboard belly. Unbidden, Kip feels a sudden rush of desire, swallowing convulsively around the big cock in his mouth.

The redhead runs toward him, raises his pistol and brings it down hard against Kip's forehead. Just like in a movie, everything goes inky black.

"Wake up, pussyboy."

Something nudges his shoulder, then pokes rudely into his ribs. Kip blinks and rolls over, wanting only to sleep.

A dream. Of course. A nightmare. How long has he been sleeping? A long, long time. It was all a bad dream. But how far back does the dream go? Back to

Kip

the day Fagan first showed up at his door? No, farther—all the way back to that long night with Zorio and Leo Battaglia, crawling naked on his hands and knees, getting fucked at both ends by gangster cock, feeling hot and ashamed, craving it, wondering what Uncle Max would think ...

All a dream. All a nightmare. He can face the morning now, knowing he'll roll out of bed into the silk robe Max bought him, pad into the kitchen nook for some espresso with Max, then head for the hotel for an honest day's work. If only he could sleep for just a few more minutes ...

"I said wake up, slutboy. The cops'll be here any minute." A hard kick in the ribs—Kip opens his eyes and stares up at Fagan's glowering face. Suddenly he remembers everything—or almost everything....

"Up, off the floor. *Now!* I'm not asking again."

Kip scrambles to his feet. If there's anything Karl Fagan has taught him, it's how to obey an order reflexively, without hesitation. Fagan throws a bundle of clothes against his chest.

"Get dressed, for chrissakes. Unless you want the cops to catch you naked again."

Kip quickly steps into his slinky panties, the shiny black pair Max loves so much. Fagan snaps his fingers impatiently. Kip dresses as fast as he can, stepping into his socks, tripping into his jeans, throwing on his T-shirt.

"Good. Now hold this." Fagan pushes a pistol into his hand. "Not like that—like you were gonna use it. Christ, don't you even know how to hold a gun? That's better. Just keep it for a while."

Kip stares dumbly at the revolver. His head is full of cobwebs. And it hurts. Now he remembers—the redhead hit him. There was a loud crack. Later there were more loud cracks, but somehow he couldn't wake up. He shakes his head, then wrinkles his brow. "Cops? Coming here? But why? You're a cop."

"I'm vice, Kippy-boy. As you ought to know. That's why I just happened to be in this sleazebag neighborhood when the incident occurred. But of course I can't file the report. I'm not Homicide."

"Homicide?" A chill runs up Kip's spine. He looks blankly around the room. "Where are they? Where did they go?"

"Who the fuck are you talking about, kid?"

"The Big Shot. And his bodyguard, the guy with the red hair—you know. And Max. Oh, no. Where's Uncle Max?"

"As if you didn't know." Fagan shoves him toward the corner. Crumpled against the wall, half-hidden behind a pile of mattresses, Max lies in a pool of blood, eyes open and staring at nothing.

"Max! Oh my God, Uncle Max!" Kip starts to rush toward the body but then recoils, unable to bear the thought of touching it. Max is beyond anyone's touch now.

"So why'd you do it, Kip?"

"Huh?" Kip's voice breaks. He stares at Fagan. Queasy. Confused. And suddenly very, very afraid.

Fagan snorts. "Don't bullshit me, pussyboy. Pretty obvious, isn't it? The old queen finally pushed you too far, didn't he? With his nasty little sex games and the frilly lace panties he'd make you wear. Not to mention renting you out to all kinds of weirdos and perverts. So tonight you finished up with your customer, Max dropped by to pick you up, and you just couldn't take it anymore. You took his gun and blew the old fartbag to kingdom come."

"What—what are you talking about?"

"It's called taking the rap, kiddo. Finally found

Kip

something you're good for besides taking a cock up your ass. Tell me the truth: Do you know who the Big Shot is?"

"No."

"Any idea at all? Where he comes from, what he does?"

"No."

"Did you see his face when you pulled off the blindfold?"

"No."

Fagan nods. "That's what we figured. Otherwise you'd be with Max over in the corner. And you didn't know a thing about Maxwell's little picture party?"

"Huh?"

"Blackmail, stupid. Max was snapping photos of the Big Shot hot-lubing your twat. Gonna make the big time. Stupid shit. And you didn't know a thing about it, did you?"

Kip can only shake his head in confusion. The look on his face is more convincing than words.

"Yeah, that's what Max kept telling us, right up to the end. Kept squealing, 'Don't hurt the boy, he doesn't know shit.' Lucky for you the Big Shot bought it. Oh, Smitty was all for putting you away permanently, but I talked 'em into a compromise plan. Namely, you keep your mouth shut and take the rap for Max's murder."

"But that's crazy."

"Better than getting your brains blown out."

"But I didn't do anything."

"Since when does that make any difference? And don't get any ideas about squirming out of it. You think I've got connections—the Big Shot's got friends in all the right places, right up to the top. We're doing you a favor, boy. You're alive, aren't you?"

Kip bites his lip and begins to cry. He looks at Max and cries harder.

"That's it. That's good. That's what I want the cops to see when they get here. Another hysterical fag hustler, gone off the deep end and killed his pimp—and now he's so sorry." Fagan can't help chuckling.

Kip grits his teeth, still crying, but feeling something more than sorrow and self-pity. It wells up inside him, fueled by Fagan's laughter. Anger. Hatred. Cold as ice.

Why does he always let them step all over him? It was fun, with Zorio. Scary, but fun, and when it was over he paid a price for it. But why does he keep having to pay and pay? Just because Karl Fagan has a big dick and the guts to slap him around, why does he always have to win? Just because the Big Shot has the power and the money, why should he go to jail?

Max is dead. They murdered him in cold blood. The only man who ever gave Kip a fair shake. Max really cared for him, and Kip cheated on him every chance he got. Now it comes to this ...

Fagan is still laughing, harder now than before. Kip stares at him through tear-filled eyes, gritting his teeth to keep them from chattering. Kip beats back the hopelessness and despair and tries to feel nothing but hate. Pure, cold hate. He can do it. He knows he can. He raises the gun, gripping it with both hands.

Fagan never stops laughing. "Come on, pussyboy. Put it down. You'll hurt yourself. We both know you're too much of a weenie to use that thing."

Kip thinks of Max. He squints and aims, hardly necessary with Fagan standing so close. Pulling the trigger takes more pressure than he thought.

Kip closes his eyes. He pulls the trigger.

And nothing happens.

He pulls again. And again. And again.

And still nothing happens, except that Fagan laughs louder. Because the revolver is empty. All six slugs are buried somewhere in Max's chest.

Fagan stops laughing. He slaps Kip so hard across the face that the boy sprawls flat on the ground.

"Get up, fagboy. Up on your knees." Kip doesn't respond. Fagan wrenches him up by a fistful of hair.

"I gotta admit, you surprised me. I never thought you'd pull the trigger. Good thing you did, though. Puts your fingerprints right where they belong." Fagan unzips his pants and reaches inside. His hand comes out full. Still the biggest. The best meal a cocksucker like Kip ever had.

"Come on, Kippy. For old time's sake. Your last chance to blow daddy. Come on, pussyboy, the homicide boys'll be here any minute. Get your mouth on it."

Kip stares at Fagan's big cock through a veil of tears. He gives up. There's no use struggling. With Fagan in his mouth he can forget everything else, at least for a little while. He opens his lips wide.

Fagan groans from sheer pleasure. "That's it, boy. Suck the big one. Damn, gonna miss that mouth of yours—finally got you trained to swallow the whole fucking thing, and Max has to go queer the deal. Only wish I had time to fuck your sweet pussy again … one last time...."

Fagan fucks, holding Kip's face in his hands. His fingers are wet with tears. "What are you crying about, cocksucker? You're gonna fit in just fine down at the state pen. Pretty piece of blond boypussy like you—the big boys'll have you pumping weights all day and choking on dick all night. Make you a sex slave. Turn you into a prison pussy. Rough guys, treat you real mean, but you like it rough, don't you, Kip?"

Fagan looks down. He can see the outline of Kip's little nub, rock-solid inside his jeans. The kid is throwing a hard-on. Fagan laughs. And then goes quiet. He can hear them on the stairs.

Fagan starts pumping, holding Kip by the hair and slam-fucking his throat. He suddenly stiffens and groans, grinding his crotch into Kip's face, plugging his cock deep in the boy's neck. His cock gives a jerk and begins to unload.

Footsteps in the hallway. Banging on the door. "Open up! Police!"

"All right, hold your horses, for chrissakes."

Fagan pulls himself from Kip's mouth, shooting the last of his load onto the boy's face. He stuffs his cock inside his pants and zips up.

He looks down at Kip. Semen dribbling from his lips. Still holding the gun. Perfect.

"Screwed again, eh, pussyboy?"

Fagan steps to the door and opens it. The cops rush in. The room, surrounded all about by mirrors, is flooded abruptly by a sea of blue.

People are talking about:

The Masquerade Erotic Book Society Newsletter

◆◆◆◆◆◆◆◆◆◆◆◆◆◆◆◆◆◆◆◆

FICTION, ESSAYS, REVIEWS, PHOTOGRAPHY, INTERVIEWS, EXPOSÉS, AND MUCH MORE!

◆◆◆◆◆◆◆◆◆◆◆◆◆◆◆◆◆◆◆◆

"I received the new issue of the newsletter; it looks better and better."
—*Michael Perkins*

"I must say that yours is a nice little magazine, literate and intelligent."
—*HH, Great Britain*

"Fun articles on writing porn and about the peep shows, great for those of us who will probably never step onto a strip stage or behind the glass of a booth, but love to hear about it, wicked little voyeurs that we all are, hm? Yes indeed...."
—*MT, California*

"Many thanks for your newsletter with essays on various forms of eroticism. Especially enjoyed your new Masquerade collections of books dealing with gay sex."
—*GF, Maine*

"... a professional, insider's look at the world of erotica ..."
—*SCREW*

"I recently received a copy of *The Masquerade Erotic Book Society Newsletter*. I found it to be quite informative and interesting. The intelligent writing and choice of subject matter are refreshing and stimulating. You are to be congratulated for a publication that looks at different forms of eroticism without leering or smirking."
—*DP, Connecticut*

"Thanks for sending the books and the two latest issues of *The Masquerade Erotic Book Society Newsletter*. Provocative reading, I must say."
—*RH, Washington*

"Thanks for the latest copy of *The Masquerade Erotic Book Society Newsletter*. It is a real stunner."
—*CJS, New York*

Free GIFT

WHEN YOU SUBSCRIBE TO:

The Masquerade Erotic Book Society Newsletter

Receive two **BADBOY** books of your choice.

Please send me **TWO BADBOY BOOKS FREE!**

1._____

2._____

☐ I've enclosed my payment of $30.00 for a one-year subscription (six issues) to: *THE MASQUERADE EROTIC BOOK SOCIETY NEWSLETTER.*

Name_____

Address_____

_____ Apt. #_____

City _____ State _____ Zip _____

Tel. ( )_____

Payment: ☐ Check ☐ Money Order ☐ Visa ☐ MC

Card No. _____

Exp. Date _____

Please allow 4–6 weeks delivery. No C.O.D. orders. Please make all checks payable to Masquerade Books, 801 Second Avenue, N.Y., N.Y., 10017. Payable in U.S. currency only.
Order by phone: 1-800-458-9640 or fax, 212 986-7355

BADBOY BOOKS
$4.95 each

JOHN PRESTON

THE ARENA 3083-0

There is a place on the edge of fantasy where every desire is indulged with abandon. Men go there to unleash beasts, to let demons roam free, to abolish all limits. At the center of each tale are the men who serve there, who offer themselves for the consummation of any passion, whose own bottomless urges compel their endless subservience.

TALES FROM THE DARK LORD 3053-9

A new collection of twelve stunning works from the man *Lambda Book Report* called "the Dark Lord of gay erotica." The relentless ritual of lust and surrender is explored in all its manifestations, in this heartstopping triumph of authority and vision from the Dark Lord!

THE HEIR • THE KING. 3048-2

The ground-breaking novel *The Heir*, written in the lyric voice of the ancient myths, tells the story of a world where slaves and masters create a new sexual society. This edition also includes a completely original work, *The King*, the story of soldier who discovers his monarch's most secret desires

MR. BENSON 3041-5

A classic erotic novel from a time when there was no limit to what a man could dream of doing.... Jamie is led down the path of erotic enlightenment by the magnificent Mr. Benson, learning to accept cruelty as love, anguish as affection, and this man as his master.

The Mission of Alex Kane

SWEET DREAMS 3062-8

It's the triumphant return of gay action hero, Alex Kane! This classic series has been revised and updated especially for Badboy, and includes loads of raw action. In *Sweet Dreams*, Alex travels to Boston where he takes on a street gang that stalks gay teenagers. Mighty Alex Kane wreaks a fierce and terrible vengeance on those who prey on gay people everywhere!

GOLDEN YEARS 3069-5

When evil threatens the plans of a group of older gay men, Kane's got the muscle to take it head on. Along the way, he wins the support—and very specialized attentions—of a cowboy plucked right out of the Old West. But Kane and the Cowboy have a surprise waiting for them....

DEADLY LIES. 3076-8

Politics is a dirty business and the dirt becomes deadly when a political smear campaign targets gay men. Who better to clean things up than Alex Kane! Alex comes to protect the dreams, and lives, of gay men imperiled by lies and deceit.

STOLEN MOMENTS 3098-9

Houston's evolving gay community is victimized by a malicious newspaper editor who is more than willing to sacrifice gays on the altar of circulation. He never counted on Alex Kane, fearless defender of gay dreams and desires everywhere.

SECRET DANGERS 111-X

Homophobia: a pernicious social ill hardly confined by America's borders. Alex Kane and the faithful Danny are called to a small European country, where a group of gay tourists is being held hostage by ruthless terrorists. Luckily, the Mission of Alex Kane stands as firm foreign policy.

LARS EIGHNER

BAYOU BOY 3084-9
Another collection of finely tuned stories from one of our finest writers. Witty and incisive, each tale explores the many ways men work up a sweat in the steamy Southwest. *Bayou Boy* also includes the "Houston Streets" stories—sexy, touching tales of growing up gay in a fast-changing world. Street smart and razor sharp, each scorching story is guaranteed to warm the coldest night!

B.M.O.C. 3077-6
A crash course in Pubic Affairs! In this college town, known as "the Athens of the Southwest," studs of every stripe are up all night—studying, naturally. In *B.M.O.C.*, Lars Eighner includes the very best of his short stories, sure to appeal to the collegian in every man. Relive university life the way it was *supposed* to be, with a cast of handsome honor students majoring in Human Homosexuality.

AARON TRAVIS

BIG SHOTS 112-8
Two fierce tales in one electrifying volume. In *Beirut*, Travis tells the story of ultimate military power and erotic subjugation; *Kip*, Travis' hypersexed and sinister take on *film noir*, appears in unexpurgated form for the first time—including the final, overwhelming chapter. Shocking and unforgettable.

BEAST OF BURDEN 105-5
Five ferocious tales from a master of lascivious prose. Innocents surrender to the brutal sexual mastery of their superiors, as taboos are shattered and replaced with the unwritten rules of masculine conquest. Hot, hard men on an erotic rampage—satisfying themselves through the unrelenting action that is a Travis trademark.

SLAVES OF THE EMPIRE 3054-7
"*Slaves of the Empire* is a wonderful mythic tale. Set against the backdrop of the exotic and powerful Roman Empire, this wonderfully written novel explores the timeless questions of light and dark in male sexuality. Travis has shown himself expert in manipulating the most primal themes and images. The locale may be the ancient world, but these are the slaves and masters of our time...." —John Preston

CLAY CALDWELL

ALL-STUD 118-7
An incredible, erotic trip into the gay future. This classic, sex-soaked tale takes place under the watchful eye of Number Ten: an omniscient figure who has decreed unabashed promiscuity as the law of his all-male land. Men exist to serve men, and all surrender to state-sanctioned fleshly indulgence. The penalties for emotion are severe, as one man discovers in this superhot thriller.

LARRY TOWNSEND

THE SCORPIUS EQUATION 3119-5
A thrilling, sex-packed science fiction adventure from the fertile imagination of Larry Townsend. Set in the far future, *The Scorpius Equation* is the story of a man caught between the twisted demands of two galactic empires. Our randy hero is required to match wits—and more—with the incredible forces that rule his world.

THE SEXUAL ADV. OF SHERLOCK HOLMES 3097-0
What Conan Doyle *didn't* know about the legendary sleuth. Holmes' most satisfying adventures, from the unexpurgated memoirs of the faithful Mr. Watson. *A Study in Scarlet* is transformed to expose Mrs. Hudson as a man in drag, the Diogenes Club as an SM arena, and clues only Sherlock Holmes could piece together. A baffling tale of sex and mystery from a master of the genre.

DEREK ADAMS

THE ADVENTURES OF MILES DIAMOND 3118-7
The hot adventures of horny P.I. Miles Diamond. 'The Case of the Missing Twin' promises to be Diamond's most rewarding case yet, packed as it is with randy studs—each with a secret or two. Miles sets about uncovering all as he tracks down the elusive and delectable Daniel Travis....

JOHN ROWBERRY

LEWD CONDUCT 3091-1
Flesh and blood men vie for power, pleasure and surrender in each of these feverish stories, and no one walks away from his steamy encounter unsated. Rowberry's men are unafraid to push the limits of civilized behavior in search of the elusive and empowering conquest.

TORSTEN BARRING

THE SWITCH 3061-X
Sometimes a man needs a good whipping, and *The Switch & Other Stories* certainly makes a case! Laced with images of men "in too-tight Levi's, with the faces of angels ... and the bodies of devils," who are imprisoned and put up to be hung and whipped, Barring's stories deliver his darkest homoerotic fantasies in the hard-boiled, no-holds-barred language of 1940s detective fiction.

CHRISTOPHER MORGAN

MUSCLE BOUND 3028-8
In the tough world of the contemporary New York City bodybuilding scene, country boy Tommy joins forces with sexy, streetwise Will Rodriguez in an escalating battle of wits and biceps at the hottest gym in the West Village.

SONNY FORD

REUNION IN FLORENCE 3070-9
Captured by Turks, Adrian and Tristan will do anything to save their heads. When Tristan is threatened by a Sultan's jealousy, Adrian begins his quest for the only man alive who can replace Tristan as the object of the Sultan's lust. Adrian's labor of love becomes a full-scale odyssey of the flesh!

EDITED BY J.A. GUERRA

MEN AT WORK 3027-X
He's the most gorgeous man you have ever seen. You yearn for his touch at night in your empty bed; but you are a man—and he's your co-worker! A collection of eight sizzling stories of man-to-man on-the-job training.

BADBOY FANTASIES 3049-0
When love eludes them—lust will do! Thrill-seeking men caught up in vivid dreams and dark mysteries—these are the brief encounters you'll pant and gasp over in B‍ADBOY *Fantasies*. Guaranteed to get you fantasizing about a beautiful B‍ADBOY of your very own!

SLOW BURN   **3042-3**
Welcome to the Body Shoppe, where men's lives cross in the pursuit of muscle. A new anthology of heated obsession and erotic indulgence. Torsos get lean and hard, pecs widen and stomachs ripple in these sexy stories of the power and perils of physical perfection.

ANONYMOUS

A SECRET LIFE   **3053-9**
Master Charles Powerscourt: only eighteen, and *quite* innocent, until his arrival at the Royal Academy, where the daily lessons are supplemented with a crash course in pure, sweet sexual heat! Banned for decades, this exuberant account of gay seduction and initiation is too hot to keep secret any longer!

SINS OF THE CITIES OF THE PLAIN   **3016-4**
Indulge yourself in the scorching memoirs of young man-about-town Jack Saul. From his earliest erotic moments with Jerry in the dark of his bedchamber, to his shocking dalliances with the lords and "ladies" of British high society, well-endowed Jack's positively *sinful* escapades grow wilder with every chapter! This Jack-of-all-trades is a sensual delight!

IMRE   *Anonymous*
What dark secrets, what fiery passions lay hidden behind strikingly beautiful Lieutenant Imre's emerald eyes? An extraordinary lost classic of fantasy, obsession, gay erotic desire, and romance in a tiny Austro-Hungarian military town on the eve of WWI.   **3019-9**

YOUTHFUL DAYS   *Anonymous*
A hot account of gay love and sex that picks up on the adventures of the four amply-endowed lads last seen in *A Secret Life*, as they explore all the possibilities of passion. Charlie Powerscourt and his friends cavort on the shores of Devon and in stately Castle Hebworth, then depart for the steamy back streets of Paris. Growing up has never been so hard!   **3018-0**

TELENY   *Anonymous*
Attributed to Oscar Wilde, *Teleny* is a strange, compelling novel, set amidst the color and decadence of *fin-de-siècle* Parisian society. A young stud of independent means seeks only a succession of voluptuous and forbidden pleasures, but instead finds love and tragedy when he becomes embroiled in an underground cult devoted to fulfilling the darkest fantasies.   **3020-2**

THE SCARLET PANSY   *Anonymous*
The great American gay camp classic! This is the story of Randall Etrange, a man who simply would not set aside his sexual proclivities and erotic desires during his transcontinental quest for true love, choosing instead to live his life to the fullest.   **3021-0**

MIKE AND ME   *Anonymous*
Mike joined the gym squad at Edison Community College to bulk up on muscle and enjoy the competition. Little did he know he'd be turning on every sexy muscle jock in southern Minnesota! Hard bodies collide in a series of workouts designed to generate a whole lot more than rips and cuts.   **3035-0**

NON-FICTION

SORRY I ASKED   *Dave Kinnick*
Unexpurgated interviews with gay porn's rank and file. How many haven't wondered what it's like to be in pictures? Dave Kinnick, longtime video reviewer for *Advocate Men*, gets personal with the men behind (and under) the "stars," and reveals the dirt and details of the porn business.   **3090-3**

THE SEXPERT *Edited by Pat Califia*

For many years now, the sophisticated gay man has known that he can turn to one authority for answers to virtually any question on the subject of man-to-man intimacy and sexual performance. Straight from the pages of *Advocate Men* comes The Sexpert! From penis size to toy care, bar behavior to AIDS awareness, The Sexpert responds to real concerns with uncanny wisdom and a razor wit.

3034-2

THE MASQUERADE LIBRARY

SECRETS OF THE CITY	03-3	$4.95
THE FURTHER ADVENTURES OF MADELEINE	04-1	$4.95
THE GILDED LILY	25-4	$4.95
PLEASURES AND FOLLIES	26-2	$4.95
STUDENTS OF PASSION	22-X	$4.95
THE NUNNERY TALES	20-3	$4.95
DEVA-DASI	29-7	$4.95
THE STORY OF MONIQUE	42-4	$4.95
THE ENGLISH GOVERNESS	43-2	$4.95
POOR DARLINGS	33-5	$4.95
LAVENDER ROSE	30-0	$4.95
KAMA HOURI	39-4	$4.95
THONGS	46-7	$4.95
THE PLEASURE THIEVES	36-X	$4.95
SACRED PASSIONS	21-1	$4.95
LUST OF THE COSSACKS	41-6	$4.95
THE JAZZ AGE	48-3	$4.95
MY LIFE AND LOVES (THE 'LOST' VOLUME)	52-1	$4.95
PASSION IN RIO	54-8	$4.95
RAWHIDE LUST	55-6	$4.95
LUSTY LESSONS	31-9	$4.95
FESTIVAL OF VENUS	37-8	$4.95
INTIMATE PLEASURES	38-6	$4.95
TURKISH DELIGHTS	40-8	$4.95
JADE EAST	60-2	$4.95
A WEEKEND VISIT	59-9	$4.95
RED DOG SALOON	68-8	$4.95
HAREM SONG	73-4	$4.95
KATY'S AWAKENING	74-2	$4.95
CELESTE	75-0	$4.95
ANGELA	76-9	$4.95
END OF INNOCENCE	77-7	$4.95
DEMON HEAT	79-3	$4.95
TUTORED IN LUST	78-5	$4.95
DOUBLE NOVEL	86-6	$6.95
LUST	82-3	$4.95
A MASQUERADE READER	84-X	$4.95
THE BOUDOIR	85-8	$4.95
SEDUCTIONS	83-1	$4.95
FRAGRANT ABUSES	88-2	$4.95
SCHOOL FOR SIN	89-0	$4.95
CANNIBAL FLOWER	72-6	$4.95
KIDNAP	90-4	$4.95
DEPRAVED ANGELS	92-0	$4.95
ADAM & EVE	93-9	$4.95
THE YELLOW ROOM	96-3	$4.95
AUTOBIOGRAPHY OF A FLEA III	94-7	$4.95
THE SWEETEST FRUIT	95-5	$4.95
THE ICE MAIDEN	3001-6	$4.95
WANDA	3002-4	$4.95
PROFESSIONAL CHARMER	3003-2	$4.95
WAYWARD	3004-0	$4.95
MASTERING MARY SUE	3005-9	$4.95
SLAVE ISLAND	3006-7	$4.95
WILD HEART	3007-5	$4.95
VICE PARK PLACE	3008-3	$4.95
WHITE THIGHS	3009-1	$4.95
THE INSTRUMENTS OF THE PASSION	3010-5	$4.95
THE PRISONER	3011-3	$4.95
OBSESSIONS	3012-1	$4.95

Title	Code	Price
MAN WITH A MAID: The Conclusion	3013-X	$4.95
CAPTIVE MAIDENS	3014-8	$4.95
THE CATALYST	3015-6	$4.95
SINS OF THE CITIES OF THE PLAIN	3016-4	$4.95
A SECRET LIFE	3017-2	$4.95
YOUTHFUL DAYS	3018-0	$4.95
IMRE	3019-9	$4.95
TELENY	3020-2	$4.95
THE SCARLET PANSY	3021-0	$4.95
THE RELUCTANT CAPTIVE	3022-9	$4.95
ALL THE WAY	3023-7	$4.95
CINDERELLA	3024-5	$4.95
THREE WOMEN	3025-3	$4.95
SLAVES OF CAMEROON	3026-1	$4.95
MEN AT WORK	3027-X	$4.95
MUSCLE BOUND	3028-8	$4.95
THE VELVET TONGUE	3029-6	$4.95
NAUGHTIER AT NIGHT	3030-X	$4.95
KUNG FU NUNS	3031-8	$4.95
SILK AND STEEL	3032-6	$4.95
THE DISCIPLINE OF ODETTE	3033-4	$4.95
THE SEXPERT	3034-2	$4.95
MIKE AND ME	3035-0	$4.95
PAULA	3036-9	$4.95
BLUE TANGO	3037-7	$4.95
THE APPLICANT	3038-5	$4.95
THE SECRET RECORD	3039-3	$4.95
PROVINCETOWN SUMMER	3040-7	$4.95
MR. BENSON	3041-5	$4.95
SLOW BURN	3042-3	$4.95
CRUMBLING FAÇADE	3043-1	$4.95
LOVE IN WARTIME	3044-X	$4.95
DREAM CRUISE	3045-8	$4.95
SABINE	3046-6	$4.95
DARLING • INNOCENCE	3047-4	$4.95
THE HEIR • THE KING	3048-2	$4.95
BADBOY FANTASIES	3049-0	$4.95
STASI SLUT	3050-4	$4.95
CAROUSEL	3051-2	$4.95
DUKE COSIMO	3052-0	$4.95
TALES FROM THE DARK LORD	3053-9	$4.95
SLAVES OF THE EMPIRE	3054-7	$4.95
MY DARLING DOMINATRIX	3055-5	$4.95
DISTANT LOVE	3056-3	$4.95
PASSAGE & OTHER STORIES	3057-1	$4.95
GARDEN OF DELIGHT	3058-X	$4.95
MASTER OF TIMBERLAND	3059-8	$4.95
TOURNIQUET	3060-1	$4.95
THE SWITCH	3061-X	$4.95
SWEET DREAMS	3062-8	$4.95
THE COMPLETE EROTIC READER	3063-6	$4.95
FOR SALE BY OWNER	3064-4	$4.95
MAN WITH A MAID	3065-2	$4.95
MISS HIGH HEELS	3066-0	$4.95
EVIL COMPANIONS	3067-9	$4.95
BAD HABITS	3068-7	$4.95
GOLDEN YEARS	3069-5	$4.95
REUNION IN FLORENCE	3070-9	$4.95
MAN WITH A MAID II	3071-7	$4.95
KATE PERCIVAL	3072-5	$4.95
HELOISE	3073-3	$4.95

MR. BENSON

JOHN PRESTON

$4.95 (CANADA $5.95) • BADBOY

Title	Code	Price
ILLUSIONS	3074-1	$4.95
THE COMPLETE *PLAYGIRL* FANTASIES	3075-X	$4.95
DEADLY LIES	3076-8	$4.95
B.M.O.C.	3077-6	$4.95
ROSEMARY LANE	3078-4	$4.95
MEMBER OF THE CLUB	3079-2	$4.95
ECSTASY ON FIRE	3080-6	$4.95
SENSATIONS	3081-4	$4.95
LOVE AND SURRENDER	3082-2	$4.95
THE ARENA	3083-0	$4.95
BAYOU BOY	3084-9	$4.95
HELLFIRE	3085-7	$4.95
THE CARNAL DAYS OF HELEN SEFERIS	3086-5	$4.95
MAUDE CAMERON	3087-3	$4.95
WOMEN AT WORK	3088-1	$4.95
VENUS IN FURS	3089-X	$4.95
SORRY I ASKED	3090-3	$4.95
LEWD CONDUCT	3091-1	$4.95
GLORIA'S INDISCRETION	3094-6	$6.95
HELEN AND DESIRE	3093-8	$4.95
SEX ON DOCTORS ORDERS	3092-X	$4.95
THE MARKET PLACE	3096-2	$4.95
THE SEXUAL ADVENTURES OF SHERLOCK HOLMES	3097-0	$4.95
STOLEN MOMENTS	3098-9	$4.95
LEATHER WOMEN	3095-4	$4.95
THE BEST OF MARY LOVE	3099-7	$4.95
LOVE'S ILLUSION	3100-4	$4.95
THE ROMANCES OF BLANCHE LA MARE	3101-2	$4.95
LADY F.	3102-0	$4.95
MANEATER	3103-9	$6.95
BEAST OF BURDEN	3105-5	$4.95
ALL-STUD	3104-7	$4.95
AN ALIZARIN LAKE READER	3106-3	$4.95
JENNIFER	3107-1	$4.95
CLAIRE'S GIRLS	3108-X	$4.95
MISTRESS MINE	3109-8	$4.95
ORF	3110-1	$6.95
SECRET DANGER (AK #5)	3111-X	$4.95
BIG SHOTS	3112-8	$4.95
AFFINITIES	3113-6	$4.95
THE PORTABLE TITIAN BERESFORD	3114-4	$4.95
SKIRTS	3115-2	$4.95
PRIVATE LESSONS	3116-0	$4.95
THE WET FOREVER	3117-9	$6.95
MILES DIAMOND	3116-7	$4.95
THE SCORPIOUS EQUATION	3119-5	$4.95

ORDERING IS EASY!

MC/VISA orders can be placed by calling our toll-free number

PHONE 800-458-9640 / FAX 212 986-7355

or mail the coupon below to:

Masquerade Books 801 Second Avenue New York, New York. 10017

BUY ANY FOUR BOOKS AND CHOOSE ONE ADDITIONAL BOOK AS YOUR FREE GIFT.

QTY.	TITLE	BS 112-8	NO.	PRICE
		SUBTOTAL		
		POSTAGE & HANDLING		
		TOTAL		

Add $1.00 Postage and Handling for tthe first book and 50¢ for each additional book. Outside the U.S. add $2.00 for the first book, $1.00 for each additional book. New York state residents add 8-1/4% sales tax.

NAME _____

ADDRESS _____ APT. # _____

CITY _____ STATE _____ ZIP _____

TEL. ( ) _____

PAYMENT: ❑ CHECK ❑ MONEY ORDER ❑ VISA ❑ MC

CARD NO. _____ EXP. DATE _____

PLEASE ALLOW 4–6 WEEKS DELIVERY. NO C.O.D. ORDERS. PLEASE MAKE ALL CHECKS PAYABLE TO MASQUERADE BOOKS. PAYABLE IN U.S. CURRENCY ONLY